Matty's War

Published by
Smith and Kraus, Inc.
Post Office Box 127, Lyme, NH 03768

First edition: December 1999
10 9 8 7 6 5 4 3 2 1

Book design by Julia Hill Gignoux, Freedom Hill Design
Illustrations and Maps by Larry Howard

Publisher's Cataloging-in-Publication Data

Thomas, Carrol.
Matty's war / by Carroll Thomas. —1st ed.
p. cm.

Summary: Two cousins share their experiences during the Civil War, both in the Simsbury, Connecticut, home of one girl, and through the letters the other writes when she goes, disguised as a boy, to fight in Virginia.

ISBN 1-57525-205-8 (cloth). —ISBN 1-57525-206-6 (paper)
1. United States—History—Civil War, 1861–1865 Juvenile fiction.
[1. United States—History—Civil War, 1861–1865 Fiction.
2. Cousins Fiction.] I. Title.

PZ7.T3656Mat 1999
[Fic]—dc21 99-36473
CIP

Matty's War

by

Carroll Thomas

A SMITH AND KRAUS BOOK

To the Reader

This book is a work of historical fiction. The main characters are imaginary, but many of the other people in the book are real. Most of the places described are real. We have based the action in the book on events that actually occurred. Most important, the character of Matty is based on the lives of women (more than 400 of them!) who really did what Matty does in this book.

Contents

Notes on Map

This map is based upon a map obtained from the Simsbury Historical Society. The map comes from the *Atlas of Hartford City and County,* dated 1869.

We have added the names of the roads as they are known today, and the houses of the fictional characters like Granny Trescott. The Allen farm, also fictional, has been located in the real Farm District. Allen Ridge is shown as a part of the real West Mountain. The original map lists several physicians and surgeons but not Dr. Godard, although he was a real person, so we have made up a house for him and his family as well. The houses of J.O. Phelps and J. Bartlett are shown just as they are on the original map.

Neely's Simsbury, 1864

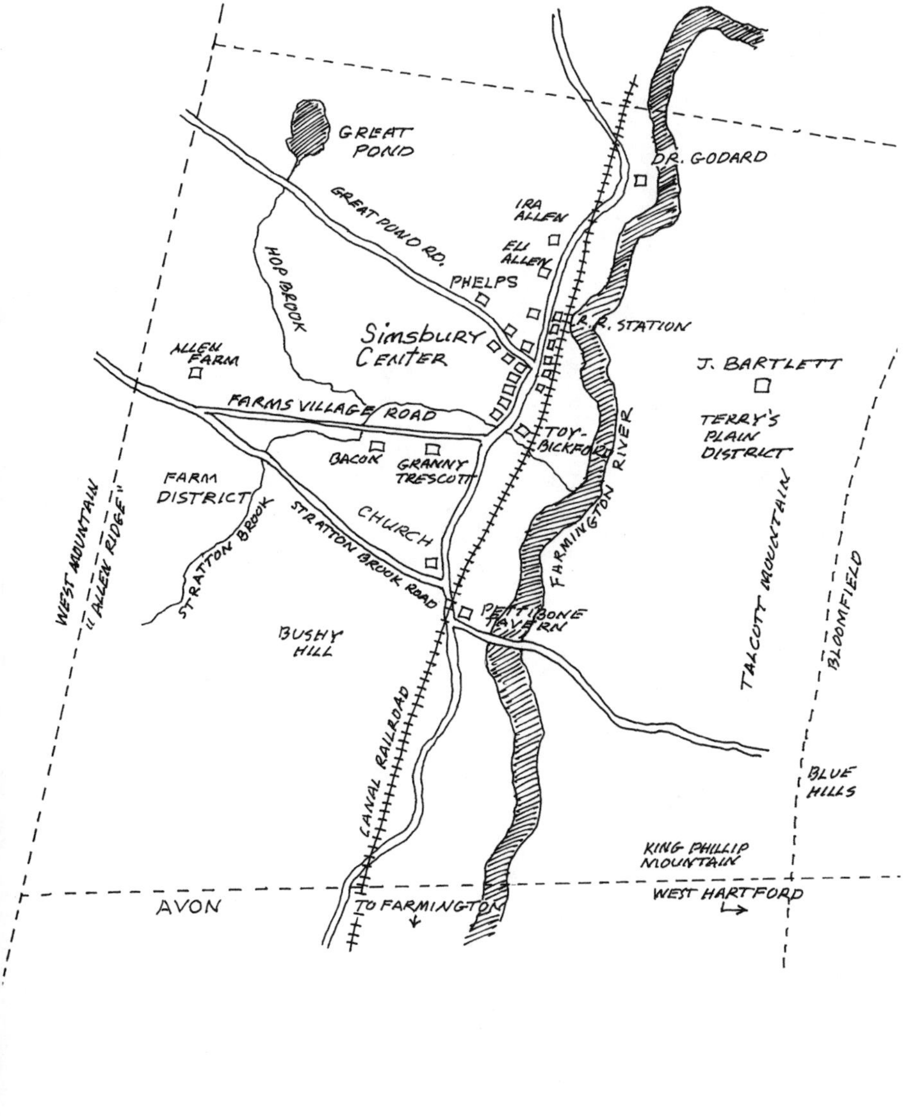

Matty's War, 1864

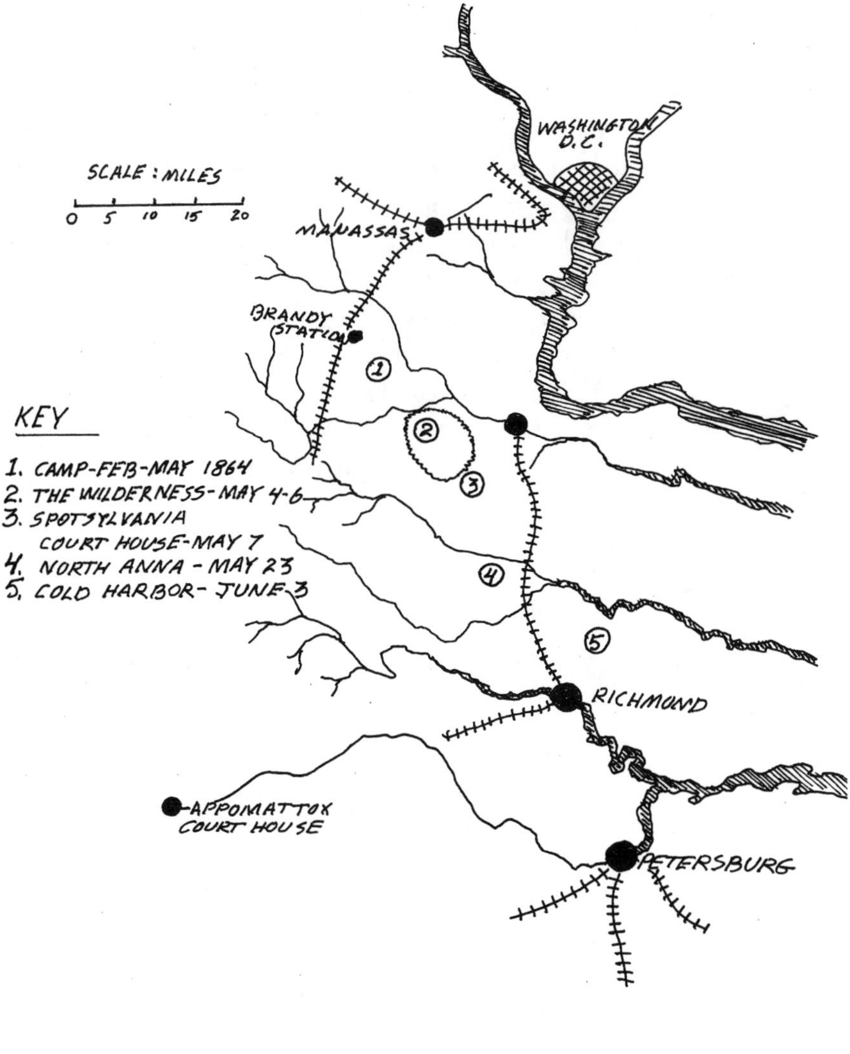
WASHINGTON D.C.
SCALE : MILES
0 5 10 15 20
MANASSAS
BRANDY STATION
KEY
1. CAMP-FEB-MAY 1864
2. THE WILDERNESS-MAY 4-6
3. SPOTSYLVANIA COURT HOUSE-MAY 7
4. NORTH ANNA - MAY 23
5. COLD HARBOR- JUNE 3
1
2
3
4
5
RICHMOND
APPOMATTOX COURT HOUSE
PETERSBURG

Note on Family Tree

Deborah Sampson (1760–1827) left a short teaching career in 1779 to enlist as a volunteer in the Massachusetts regiment of the American army in the Revolutionary War. Under the name of Robert Shurtleff, she fought in several battles with the Continental forces. Wounded and hospitalized, she was given an honorable discharge. In 1785, she married and subequently had three children. In addition to pursuing a speaking tour of her military experiences, she anonymously published her memoirs, *The Female Review*, in 1797. She also received both federal and state pensions for her military service. Although Deborah Sampson is real, her relationship to the Allen family is purely fictitious.

Neely's and Matty's Family Tree

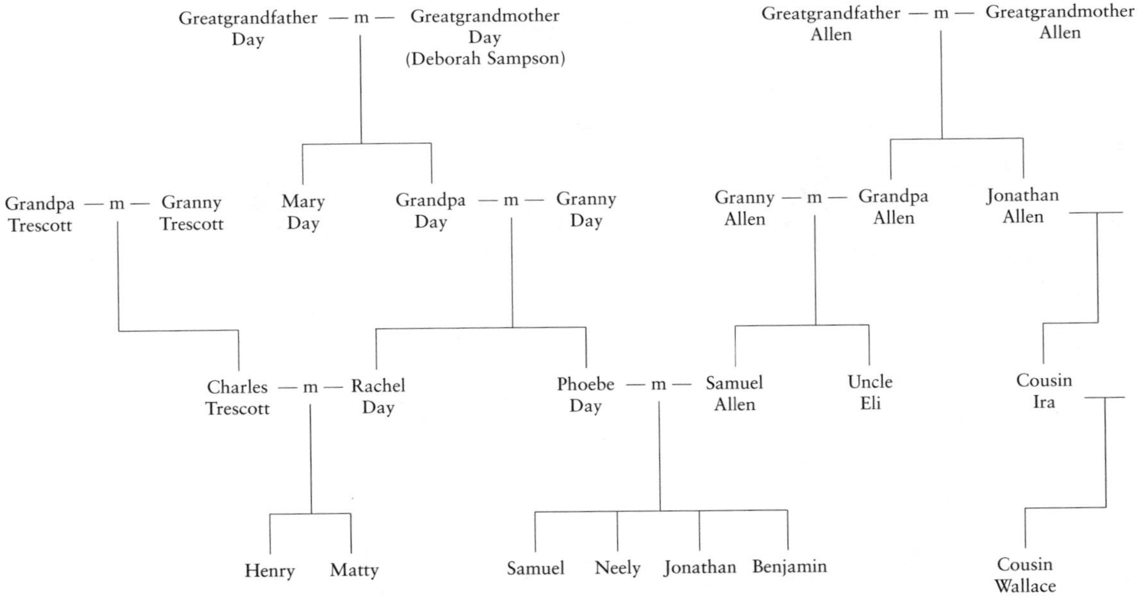

CHAPTER ONE

"Matty's Coming!"

"Matty's coming! Matty's coming!" It was all I could think about. Standing in the ice-cold barn loading up the sleigh with warm blankets, the words filled my head like a joyous song. It was December, almost Christmas, and Matty's coming to live with us was the best gift of all.

Not everyone was pleased about my cousin's arrival.

"There'll be some changes around here now," Mother had said, putting down Matty's letter and slipping her reading glasses into the pocket of her apron. "Oh, I loved my sister Rachel, God rest her soul, and I miss her terribly.

But that little girl of hers was always such a package of mischief! So different from you, Cornelia. You were a leaf-turner." The clacking rhythm of her knitting needles punctuated her speech. "Even when you were just a year old, I could put you down in a pile of autumn leaves, and you would sit and pick up a leaf, look at it, turn it over, put it down, pick up the next leaf, and amuse yourself. If Rachel put Matty down in the same pile, she'd brush the leaves aside and crawl off to explore somewhere else! Turn your head one minute and she'd be climbing into the corn crib. I never knew such a child!"

Father had looked up from his paperwork. "Now, Phoebe, Matty's sixteen. Probably grown to be a nice young lady by now. She'll be good company for Neely. Life on a farm isn't easy for a girl with three brothers."

"Probably get Neely into trouble," sniffed Samuel, the oldest of my brothers. He had never forgiven Matty for pushing him into Stratton Brook six years ago. "She's trouble, Father. Bound to be a bad influence on Jonathan and Benjamin."

I suppose that introductions are in order. My name is Cornelia Allen, although almost everyone — except my mother — calls me Neely. My parents own a farm in Simsbury, Connecticut, where my family has lived for the last two hundred years. Father often says the Simsbury soil grows Allens best! Matty is really Matilda Trescott, my sixteen-year-old cousin, who moved with her parents and older brother, Henry, to Kansas Territory when she was ten.

It wasn't a lucky move. Their farm did poorly and there was constant danger from pro-slavery raiders from Missouri. After a few years, Aunt Rachel died of the measles, leaving Uncle Charles to take care of the farm and my two cousins. Now with the War of the Rebellion going on, Kansas had become an even worse place to live — a few months ago, Confederate raiders had crossed the border from Missouri and burned the town of Lawrence, not far from Uncle Charles' farm. Father said this was in retaliation for the Union victories at Gettysburg and Vicksburg.

Matty's last letter had told how their farm had been burned, and that Uncle Charles and Cousin Henry were now joining the Union army. There was nothing for Matty to do except return to Connecticut and live with us in Simsbury, until the war ended. At least this terrible war was bringing some good to us!

Now, just two weeks later, Jonathan and I were helping Father hitch up the horse and sleigh to meet Matty at the train depot. What would she look like? Would I recognize her? Would she still be my closest friend?

CHAPTER TWO

Reunion

Standing on the platform in the frigid night air, we waited for what seemed like hours. When the train finally arrived and the smoke cleared, I immediately spotted her standing by one of the doors. I needn't have worried about recognizing Matty. I knew my cousin right away — there is no one else quite like her!

She'd grown taller than me by almost half a head. Her long, curly black hair was tied back with a piece of string — Matty never did worry much about appearances. Living on the frontier had made her care even less about fashion. She was bundled up in a plain black woolen cloak, with a scarf and mittens made of the same fabric. A coarse brown skirt peeped out from under the cloak. No hoop skirts for her!

Was she beautiful? Of course I thought so, but a more objective observer would have called her "striking" or "handsome." Her face had lost its girlish roundness. I could see that she had attracted the attention of several of the men standing on the platform, the result of the spirited discussion she was engaged in as she stepped down from the train.

"Well, I certainly think so! General Grant would be a good choice!" she was saying to the distinguished gentleman who'd preceded her down the steps and was offering his arm. Matty was balancing two tattered bags.

"Really, Miss Trescott, I can take those for you," said the man whom I recognized as the local surgeon, Wharton Godard.

"But then, not everyone agrees that — why it's Cousin Neely! Darling Neely!" she cried as she threw her arms around me. "And Jonathan, is this little Jonathan? How happy I am to see you all!" Jonathan blushed at the enthusiastic hug, but a smile lit up his dark eyes.

"Welcome home Matty," Father said, scooping up the bags. "And good evening, Dr. Godard. I'm pleased to see you home for the holidays. I hope my niece hasn't been talking your ear off."

"I met brave Dr. Godard when we were changing trains in New Haven. He's just returned from his hospital unit in Virginia, and we've been talking about the War."

"Hello, Dr. Godard," I said. "Is someone meeting you here?"

"Yes, Miss Allen, I expect Thomas should be here soon. Why yes, here's my son now!" At this, a tall, handsome young man strode up from behind us and greeted his father warmly. After a friendly nod and smile, Tom stared admiringly at Matty. Hastily, I made the necessary introductions.

"Pleased to meet you, Tom," she said, green eyes flashing. There was silence as he continued to stand there, eyes fixed on her. Matty met his stare. She had the same dark eyebrows, determined chin and high forehead she'd had as a girl — the same features that Ma and Aunt Rachel and so many of the Day women seemed to have. Although Samuel had often teased Matty about having eyes that were "like a cat," those amber-flecked eyes were her most striking feature.

"Well," I broke in, "it surely is too cold to stand here on the platform." Jonathan, who had been stamping his feet to keep warm, nodded in agreement. "I'm sure we'll see you both in town soon," said Father. "Give my Christmas greetings to Mrs. Godard and your family." Then Father turned to us and signaled toward the sleigh. "Your mother's holding dinner." I grabbed Matty's arm and pulled her with me toward the sleigh. The two of us crunched through the snow, laughing, while Jonathan ran ahead.

"Well, you certainly seemed to interest young Tom Godard!" I said.

"He looks interesting too," she laughed as we climbed under the blankets and readied ourselves for the ride. "But why isn't he off in the War? He looks old enough. Never mind — how are *you*, Neely? You look lovely as ever. And with your hair piled up like that, you look so grown up."

"I am grown up, Matty. I've finished district school and will be going off to the Seminary in Hartford in a few months. Now that you're here, perhaps Pa will send you too. It would be wonderful to be classmates again!"

Matty smiled. "Perhaps we will be, Neely."

Jonathan, up front with Pa, called out a warning as he clicked the reins, but we both fell backwards as the team clopped off into the black night.

"What's so special about this Seminary, Neely?"

"It's just for women, Matty! It's a chance for us to get as good an education as Samuel! It was started by Catharine Beecher, the sister of the famous author, Harriet Beecher Stowe."

"What would we study?"

I was happy to note that it was "we" already. But before I could answer, Matty was exclaiming over the moonlit, snow-covered elms that lined the streets of Simsbury. Just as quickly, she turned the conversation to her trip from Kansas: a bumpy week by stagecoach to

St. Louis, and four days on the train, with many changes and long waits. She'd arrived this morning in New Haven, to catch the Canal Railroad north to Simsbury.

I didn't care where the conversation went. I was so happy to have Matty back with us. There would be plenty of time later to talk about school and Tom Godard and Simsbury.

CHAPTER THREE

At Allen Farm

Though it was almost eight P.M. when the horses turned in at our gate, Ma had a huge dinner waiting for us. I think she meant it as a welcome home, but I think she also wanted to let everyone know that Matty's arrival wasn't going to upset things around the farm.

"A body's got to eat," she'd said that morning, "and poor Matty will be starved after such a long trip. I imagine she's not had a decent meal in ages, what with Rachel gone, and living out there in the wilderness with no woman around to take care of her."

"Now Phoebe, it's not like they've been living with savages," Pa had replied. "Kansas is just frontier, that's all. From what they wrote, their cabin was big enough and I'm sure that Charles provided for her."

"Well, food and shelter is one thing, but there are other things in this world. Womanly things. That girl was trouble enough when she was ten and had a mother. Lord only knows what she's like now. I want to start her off right. Let her know that our home is open to her. She is family, after all."

When we entered the kitchen, the warmth of the stove greeted us like a blast of cheer. The aroma of roast turkey, potatoes, yams, and pies thrilled our senses and excited our appetites. We all would have liked to huddle in the kitchen enjoying the moment, but Ma shooed us away. Removing our boots and hanging our cloaks and scarves by the fire, we were whisked off to the dining room and seated at the overflowing table.

"Oh, Aunt Phoebe, it looks like a holiday feast! I can't remember when I last had turkey, and fresh turnip! What a treat! It really is too much. Everything looks wonderful."

"The apple pie is mine," laughed Jonathan, eyeing Matty warily. "And the blueberry and pumpkin, too."

"Oh, look . . . This can't be Baby Benjamin, now can it?" exclaimed Matty, as my seven-year-old brother walked in, carefully carrying a bowl of walnuts. "You were just a little thing when I left. You probably don't remember me at all."

"Well, I thought I did, but now I'm not so sure," replied my rosy-cheeked little brother. Turning, he yelled into the parlor, "Hey, Samuel, you were wrong. She's not ugly and her skin's not green like a frog!"

Grinning, Samuel swaggered into the room. "Yes, it is, Benny, she's just hiding it. Hello Matilda. Welcome back to civilization. How is life among the savages?" Despite the challenging gleam in his blue eyes, I think he was secretly glad to see Matty again.

"The only savages in Kansas are the ones who keep slaves," she retorted, "but we are chasing them back into Arkansas and Missouri where they came from. And I see that you haven't changed one bit, Samuel Allen! Maybe a soldier's uniform would improve your manners."

"Shows how much you know," said Samuel. I hated his superior tone. "I am studying at Yale. No war for me."

"What's all this war talk before dinner? Come on, now — I'm starving. Let's eat!" Pa's booming voice silenced everyone except Benjamin, who was busy staking his claim to the largest drumstick. The beauty of Ma's best china plates and damask tablecloth was soon lost in the clatter of knives and forks and the happy sounds of feasting.

Jonathan was filling his plate for the third time and Pa was sipping his coffee when a knock at the back door interrupted our meal. Pa got up and opened the door.

"Isaiah, come in. What has you out on this cold and bitter night? Have you had your supper? We're just in the dining room, please join us." Ma already had an extra plate out and was busy shuffling the boys to make room for our visitor.

Our neighbor stomped the snow from his worn boots and entered the dining room. "Oh yes, Mr. Allen. I ate earlier. No, don't you bother, Miss Allen, I can't stay but a minute. I've been over at the Coopers' seeing to their sick mare. They just heard this afternoon that their boy Billy was killed at a place called Mine Run in Virginia. It happened two weeks ago, but they only now got word."

"That's terrible news, terrible," Pa said. "Poor Mrs. Cooper. Isaiah, will you at least have some coffee? Sit down by the fire and warm up a bit. Phoebe, get some coffee for . . . "

Ma looked pale, but she was already rustling the cups and saucers. Every face in the room was somber, silent. Isaiah's strong brown eyes and dark skin glistened in the warmth of the room.

"No, I'd better get on home. It's late and I have to get up early. Thanks anyway. But I should say hello to the visitor from Kansas I've been hearing so much about. Welcome to Simsbury, Miss Trescott." Before anyone could say a word, he turned and disappeared into the night.

"Who was that?" Matty asked. "I didn't know there were any freed blacks living in Simsbury. Is he a runaway?"

"That is Isaiah," bristled Samuel. "He lives over by the creek in our old summer cabin. He sometimes works for us, and he makes a good living tending sick animals. He is a good friend and not a runaway. He's as free as any man here in Simsbury."

Pa cast a long look at Ma, who began clearing. Jonathan fidgeted in his seat and I knew I had to change the subject.

"So sad about Bill Cooper," I said. "Such a nice young man."

"Only a year older than Samuel, too," added Ma. "I am glad that we don't have to worry about any of us Allens being in the war."

"I'm proud of my Pa and brother Henry fighting in the war!" exclaimed Matty. "I don't see how you can all sit back and do nothing while . . . "

"Matty, we are doing our part," interrupted Pa gently. "We grow food for the soldiers and we buy government bonds. Someone has to keep the home fires burning. War isn't all battles and fighting."

"And Ma and Pa have worked with the Abolition Society for years," added Jonathan.

"But it's not the same, not the same as fighting, I mean . . . "

"Matilda dear," said Ma in her softest firm voice. "We know that you are proud of your father and Henry, and worried about them too. Here we are all family, and everyone at this table is proud of what they are doing." She looked seriously at the rest of us. "I'm sorry I didn't think before I spoke. None of us can imagine what it would be like to have Confederate raiders attack our farm, and none of us can imagine how we would feel if Allen farm were burned to the ground. You have seen the war and understand what it is about better than we do. Living here in Connecticut, far from the fighting in Virginia and in the West, makes us too comfortable sometimes. Perhaps your being here with us will give us a new outlook on things, Matty."

She got up and reached for her apron. "Cornelia, you take charge of cleaning up. I'd better make plans to go and visit Sarah Cooper in the morning. Jonathan, that means you will have to get up early and chop me some extra kindling. I need to make a pie and some biscuits to take along."

Suddenly, the feasting was over, and the house was abuzz with new energies. So ended the first meal that Matty shared with us.

CHAPTER FOUR

Christmas

Christmas on the farm was always a blur of activity, and the next several days passed quickly. Matty and I spent all our time together, helping Ma with the cooking and baking, stringing popcorn to decorate the house, and amusing little Benjamin with stories of Saint Nicholas. It was so good to have Matty back in Simsbury that soon it began to feel as if she had never left. Everyone was caught up in the spirit of the season, and the house smelled of gingerbread and mincemeat, Christmas candles and pine boughs.

It had been unusually cold. Pa and Samuel were busy cutting ice up at Great Pond and hauling it to our icehouse, so it fell to Matty, Jonathan, and me to cut our Christmas tree. On the day of Christmas Eve we set out after breakfast to climb West Mountain in search of a Scotch pine I had found last July. A fresh dusting of snow had fallen during the night, giving the mountain a glistening, magical look.

"Slow down, you two," shouted Jonathan. "The trees aren't going anywhere."

"I know," I called back, "but I can't help myself. The woods are so beautiful. This day was made for a walk on the mountain. Everything is just perfect — the day, the snow, and our Christmas tree. You'll see. It's just perfect!"

"That's fine," he interrupted, "but a walk in the woods isn't a foot race. I declare, it's as if you two were trying to lose me." With that, he began to trot, his long legs effortlessly carrying him along. It only took a glance and a smile from Matty to set us off. In an instant the three of us were sprinting through the orchard as if our lives depended on it.

When we reached the top of Allen Ridge, we were out of breath. Matty and Jonathan had finished dead even, with me lagging seriously behind. In spite of the cold and snow we threw ourselves on the ground, gasping for breath and giggling. The cold crisp air burned my lungs and throat.

"I had forgotten how lovely the view is," cried Matty. "Simsbury is one of the most beautiful places on earth!"

Allen Ridge isn't the official name of the ridge, but since it stands behind our farm, we Allens have taken to calling it after ourselves. From the top, you can see the entire valley, north to Granby, south to Avon and east to King Philip Mountain. I stood for a moment, looking down at the slender thread meandering through the snow. I knew it to be Stratton Brook, twisting and turning its way eastward to the Farmington River.

The countryside was dotted with barns and farmhouses, crisscrossed with dark ribbons of roads, and decorated with snow-covered fenceposts. Off in the distance, we could see the town itself, huddled beside the Farmington River and bisected north to south by the Canal Railroad.

"Oh look, you can see the new train station and Cousin Ira's store, and that grey house must be the Bacons'," said Matty happily. "And there is Granny Trescott's and the old Pettibone Tavern. Hopmeadow Street hasn't really changed that much. And look, Neely, you can still see some of the old Canal. Do you think we could go skating on it like we used to?"

"We'll ask Pa to take us when he goes to town next Saturday for the mail." But I noticed that Matty wasn't listening.

"The one thing I really missed in Kansas was the view from up here. Everything there is so flat and uninteresting." Looking over at me, she grinned and hastily added,

"Oh, and of course I missed you, Neely. Even with the changes, Simsbury still looks the way I remembered it."

"The changes you're thinking about live in the big brownstone house, the last one on Hopmeadow Street," teased Jonathan. "Tom Godard's. I'm sure he will be going to the Christmas party at the Phelps'." He raised his arms as if he were waltzing and began to swing back and forth, shuffling his felt boots through the crusty snow. He seemed quite proud to know about Tom Godard.

"Oh, don't be silly," said Matty. "I don't care anything about some city boy moldering in school when he ought to be in uniform like his father! How a brave man like Dr. Godard could have such a son is beyond me. If I were a boy, I'd . . . " Her voice trailed off.

With the mention of the War, we all paused. I remembered what Ma had said about Henry and Uncle Charles, and tried to imagine what I would feel like if Pa and Samuel were off fighting the Rebels. Jonathan looked at the ground and shifted his weight from foot to foot. We were all learning from our new relationships with Cousin Matty, and some of the lessons were hard ones.

The silence was shattered by Matty's clear voice. "Yes, it is beautiful. Very beautiful. I know this place. I can name every house and business. Oh, look, you can even see the Phelps' house! But what is that large building there past Granny Trescott's?"

"That's Toy-Bickford, the gunpowder fuse factory,"

said Jonathan proudly. "Since the War started, it's really grown. Making big profits, I hear."

"Don't talk to me of war profiteering, Jonathan Allen, or I'll throw you down the hill! My Pa and brother are off fighting, like real men, for the Union!"

He picked up a handful of powdery snow, and flicked it gently into Matty's face. "There. That should cool you off and slow you down. I just meant that our little town has been growing since you've been gone — that's all!"

"Let's not spoil this lovely day with war talk," I pleaded. "Christmas is a time for celebration. Jonathan, don't you start trouble or I'll tell Pa. Matty, we'll say a special prayer for Henry and Uncle Charles tonight in church. Now let's get a move on. If someone else has taken my Scotch pine, I will hold you both responsible."

The next morning we were all awakened early by Benjamin, who was eager to see what delights Saint Nicholas had brought to Allen farm. He was not disappointed. A new sled had been leaning against the hearth when he awoke, and he was dressed and out in the orchard even before breakfast. The rest of us were happily unwrapping our new mittens and woolen hats and scarves, fresh fruits and candies and new felt boots. I had just opened a new diary when Pa handed me a large box.

"Ransom's Department store? When were you in Hartford? Oh, Pa, a new cloak! How did you know?"

Pa smiled and winked at Ma. "A young lady must

look her best at the Seminary, you know." He handed Matty a similar box.

"Matty, you got one too! Now we shall look like sisters. Isn't it grand?"

"We want you to look your best at Seminary, too, Matty," Pa beamed. "We've decided to send you to Hartford with Neely."

I ran to Pa and threw my arms around his neck. "Oh Pa, that's the best Christmas present of all!"

"Thank you, Uncle Samuel, Aunt Phoebe. The cloak is beautiful. I don't know what to say. Thank you." She got up and left the room.

I started after her, but Ma caught me by the hand. "Leave her be," she said softly. "That girl needs some time by herself today. It's not easy being so far from loved ones on Christmas, especially with the War going on."

I smiled and nodded. "Maybe the Phelps' party will cheer her up. We'll be the envy of all Simsbury in our new finery."

"Maybe it will," said Ma. "Maybe. Still, something is troubling that girl. Like she's trying to figure something out. Why I . . . BENJAMIN!"

Turning toward the open door, I stared in disbelief. There stood a snow-covered, golden-haired cherub faintly resembling my little brother.

"Benjamin Aaron Allen, what happened to you? You're covered with snow. You march right back out on that porch and strip down to your woolies, young man. I declare!"

As Ma rushed off to clean up the melting snow and salvage Benjamin's wet clothes, I settled into her rocker by the fire and tried to regain the Christmas spirit by starting my new diary. Ma was right. Something was weighing on Matty's mind. I decided it would be up to me to find out what.

CHAPTER FIVE

The Phelps' Party

The next evening found our household a flurry of excitement and confusion. The Phelps' Christmas party was the biggest social event of the holiday season, of the whole year really, and everyone was eager to go. The seven of us all wanted to look our best.

Matty and I were just putting the finishing touches on our outfits when Ma came bursting into our room.

"You girls had better hurry or . . . oh my, don't you both look lovely! Did I say girls? Oh no, I should say young ladies. Matty, I hardly recognize you so dressed up. You do look so much like your Ma — a true Day woman through and through." Ma smiled and paused next to my dresser. "And Neely, your new cloak sets off your yellow hair and blue eyes just fine. Pa is going to be so pleased to see both of you, looking so grown-up and pretty! Two young ladies, ready for the ball!"

"More like two scarecrows in the worst of a windstorm," Samuel commented derisively, poking his blond head through the doorway. "Be careful not to frighten off the boys there, Cousin Matt. Be sure to stay in the corner or that Tom what's-his-name will . . . "

Samuel was not allowed to finish, as Ma waved him off with a look that would have frightened even a crow. But the magic of the evening could not be shattered even by Samuel's foolish rantings. Matty looked beautiful, even serene, and we were headed to the Phelps' party in style.

We did not ride in the sleigh, as it was too crowded with all the food Ma had prepared. Pa drove the sleigh, and the rest of us clambered up on the big farm wagon. Samuel and Isaiah had spread hay in the wagon bed and covered that with blankets for us to sit on. We settled in the back, wrapping ourselves in additional blankets. The long ride down to Simsbury was a warm one, filled with anticipation.

"I am going to eat all the chocolate I can find," proclaimed little Benjamin. "The Phelps always have such fine candies and cakes."

"Not as fine as Ma's pies," I put in.

"I shall play my fiddle with the band," added Jonathan. "Mr. Phelps told me last year that I was the most promising young musician in all of Simsbury."

"You just want to impress Sally Randall," I teased. "I know all about that.

"Jonny's fiddle sounds like the devil singin' off key," teased Isaiah, "But I'm with you, Benjy. The food's the finest at the Phelps', next to your mother's, that is."

"Whoever is playing the music, I shall dance with every pretty young lady in town," boasted Samuel. "When the sun comes up tomorrow, every one of them will be thinking of me."

"Then you had better be prepared to dance with Neely and Matty," said Isaiah. "I don't think you'll find two prettier anywhere."

"Well, he'll have to stand in line to dance with Matty. I believe her dance card is already filled up by Tom Godard. Of course, Neely will probably be free all evening."

"You hush, Jonathan!" exclaimed Matty. "Neely will have all the heads turning tonight, you can be sure of that. As for me, I'd prefer talking to Aunt Mary to strutting about like a peacock." Jonathan and Samuel started to protest at the same time, and Ma tried to quiet them both.

At that moment, Isaiah clicked the horses into a trot and started a song. Between the bouncing and the music we were soon all singing and laughing. When we turned from Hopmeadow Street, the Phelps' house lit up the dark night. It was an ordinary house, like many other white frame houses in Simsbury — with one exception: Old Captain Phelps had built his house with a grand ballroom. The older folks always said it had been used for meetings, but for us, the Phelps' ballroom was part of Simsbury's Christmas tradition.

As we climbed the narrow stairs and entered the great hall, we were overcome with the excitement of the party. The room was transformed into a maze of tables and food, with one empty corner reserved for the musicians. Everywhere we looked there were people we knew. It was hard to take even a few steps without someone stopping to wish us a happy holiday or starting a conversation about one thing or another. Sadly, some of Simsbury's young men were missing. The War was reaching us, even here. We did see many of our relatives — Aunt Mary Day, our east-of-the-river Allen cousins, and Cousin Ira. Matty sat in a corner for a long time talking to Granny Trescott.

At exactly seven, the musicians began tuning up. Soon the room was filled with sounds of a quadrille, rather fast music for which there is a lively dance. Some people began to pair off and the rest of us faded back to give the dancers room to move. The music seemed to be a signal for the younger children to gravitate toward the dessert tables, while the older men shifted toward the side yard, relieved to escape into the cold night air to smoke their pipes and talk about farming, business, and politics.

Eventually I drifted over to where Matty was sitting

with Aunt Mary Day, our great-aunt and sister to our grandfather. Matty was dabbing her eyes with a square of embroidered linen. Then I saw her wrap something in her handkerchief. Knowing how close Mary had been to Matty's mother, I decided not to interrupt. I sat down a few seats away and boldly tapped my foot to the music. I was startled a few minutes later when Matty came over and sat down beside me.

"I see that you have been catching up with Aunt Mary and Granny Trescott. Is everything all right?" I asked.

"Yes, I'm fine now. Aunt Mary has always been the one I could turn to, the one I could trust. Besides you, she is the one person I can share secrets with. But she looks much older than she did before I left. It reminds me of how much time has passed." Matty sighed, then forced a smile. "Look at everyone having such a wonderful time. You were right to make me come, Neely. Now if we could only find your Prince Charming . . . " She winked.

She had a strange look on her face, but before I could question her, I spotted Dr. Godard across the room. Behind him stood Tom, dapper and handsome in a new blue suit. I was about to comment when I was interrupted by my cousin Wallace, Ira Allen's seventeen-year-old son.

"My Ma says I should ask you to dance since you look so pretty and all," he said, his lanky frame and pale face making him look a little silly. Not that I really cared about such things, but I did not want to be seen dancing my first, and maybe only, dance with my storekeeper cousin if I could help it.

"Why thank you, Wallace. It is really very sweet of you and your mother to think of me, but . . . "

"Cornelia," he sniffed, "you know perfectly well that it is extremely rude for a young lady to refuse an invitation to dance when asked by a proper young gentleman, even when that gentleman is her second cousin."

"Especially when it is her second cousin," added Matty. She made a face at me as I stood up and took Wallace's arm. As we walked to the center of the room, I felt as if all eyes were focused on me. I did not know if my feet would be able to move at first, but somehow Wallace was able to get us going and soon I was lost in the music. Wallace or not, dancing was wonderful.

After two dances with my skinny cousin, I made excuses and went to talk with Cousin Ira and his wife Sarah. Out of the corner of my eye, I saw Wallace making a beeline for Matty, and I chuckled to myself.

"Where did you get that cloak I saw you wearing?" Cousin Sarah pulled me back to the conversation.

"Why, it was a Christmas gift," I replied.

"Certainly not bought in Simsbury," sniffed Cousin Ira as he began a tirade about losing business to big city stores. A few minutes later, seeing Matty heading for the side door, I sought relief in her company. I caught up with her on the terrace.

"How did you like dancing with Cousin Wallace?" I

teased. "He is so strange! But a good dancer, I'm surprised to say."

"For your information, I did not dance with him. I was suddenly stricken with a fierce headache and had to beg his forgiveness." On the word "forgiveness," her voice shot up an octave and she broke into a giggle. "Besides, I have other things on my mind."

"Yes, I know you've been thinking about something. Will you tell me about it?" I looked hopefully into her clear green eyes.

"Of course, Neely. It's just that this is neither the time nor the place. You will have to swear, absolutely swear, that you will guard my secret with your life."

"Oh, Matty, of course I will! Just knowing you will share your secret with me is enough."

She smiled at me, a strange sort of smile. "Just so you don't forget. Sometimes surprises can upset you. But that's enough for now — let's walk a little. The night air feels good after the stuffiness of the party and Cousin Wallace."

CHAPTER SIX

Copperheads

As we ambled along the path to the side yard, we could hear the men talking on the porch, so we slowed our pace. When we could hear clearly, I started to turn and head back, but Matty grabbed my arm and sat down quickly on the stone wall bordering the path.

"Matty, this wall is covered with snow. It's too cold to . . . "

"Shhh, keep your voice down. I want to hear." The look on her face showed that she was determined to eavesdrop.

"That is nonsense, plain nonsense!" came the gruff voice. "If you ask me, this war is lost, and that Lincoln ought to be arrested! How many thousands of our boys have died and for what? Fighting other Americans who want peace and prosperity, the same as us! Hogwash and nonsense!"

I knew by the nasal tone that the speaker was Joseph Bartlett, who lived across the river at Terry's Plain. Pa had said that Mr. Bartlett was a Democrat and that he held some strong views. At the beginning of the War, Mr. Bartlett and his friends had been called Peace Democrats, but soon many people in Simsbury had taken to calling them "Copperheads," like the snake. Instead of being insulted, the Peace Democrats had taken it as a badge of honor.

"Who is that awful man?" whispered Matty indignantly.

It was my turn to shush Matty. "Keep your voice down. That's just Mr. Bartlett, letting off steam."

I was surprised to hear Dr. Godard's voice replying.

"You are certainly entitled to your opinion, Bartlett, but I hate to hear such talk about the President. His courage and leadership have been essential these last three years. He's fighting to protect our Union, our country, our way of life. Those Rebels, so wedded to their slaves and brutality, should be jailed as traitors."

For a moment the men all seemed to speak at once, some agreeing with Mr. Bartlett, some with Dr. Godard.

"The only treason, sir, is the unlawful taking of another man's property. Our country, our Constitution, is based on this one principle — property rights. And your vile Mr. Lincoln has proclaimed his intention, illegally and unconstitutionally, to confiscate all the slaves in the South and set them free. That, sir, is several million slaves, worth billions of dollars. Billions! And by what right? None, I tell you. None!"

"Just a minute there, Bartlett." I was shocked to hear Pa's voice echoing clearly in the night. "You're entitled to your opinion of this war, but to claim any legal right for one man to own another is completely immoral. Mr. Lincoln is only doing what is just." I could hear several of the men murmuring in agreement.

"Allen, you are not one to talk. When they start locking up all of those responsible for this thievery, your name will be high on the list. Don't think that some people in town don't know about you and your hired hand, that runaway Elijah or whatever Christian name he took when he arrived here. Free blacks don't just suddenly appear in town without a reason. And don't think I don't know about your Jayhawking brother-in-law in Kansas — and the rest of your abolitionist relatives! For my money, I say lock them all up — runaway slaves and those who protect them as well! The rest of us would be better off."

Up to this point, I had been afraid that Matty would lose her temper and interrupt, but after hearing this threat against Pa and Isaiah, I found myself bursting toward them.

"Neely, wait! You can't . . . " But Matty was too late.

Waves of anger poured over me as I rushed into the circle of men, shouting and waving my arms at Mr. Bartlett. He stood frozen, too startled to move or speak.

"Jayhawking! Runaways!" I shouted. "I'll show you, you Copperhead snake in the grass! If you ever come near Allen farm, or Isaiah, I'll lock *you* up! In the barn with the other animals, where you belong!"

Suddenly there were arms around my waist, dragging me away. When we got to the end of the hedge, Pa deposited me on a garden bench.

"Cornelia, what's gotten into you?" The calmness in his voice was a welcome surprise. "It's a good thing your mother wasn't here to see this. Let's hope she doesn't hear about it."

I couldn't believe my father was asking me not to tell Ma. Waves of relief flooded over me.

"Oh, Pa, I couldn't help myself. One minute we were just sitting there listening, and the next that man was saying those awful things about you and Isaiah. You don't really think anyone would ever take him, do you? He's not a runaway, is he? That's just a lot of talk, isn't it? Pa?"

"Don't you worry about Isaiah. He's as free as you or I, Neely, and will stay in Simsbury as long as he wants to. Now why don't you girls go inside and warm up? Find yourselves some handsome young men to dance with. I think I'll find Ma and have a dance myself."

Minutes later, Matty and I were standing by the fireplace in the great room, warming our backs and talking with some of the other girls. From the conversation, it seemed to me that most of my friends had spent the better part of the evening dancing, while I had spent mine sitting on a snow-covered wall and making a fool of myself.

My thoughts were interrupted by a polite cough. I looked up to see Tom Godard and another young man standing in front of me, smiling broadly.

"Good evening, Neely," said Tom. "Have you met my good friend Stuart Deming from Farmington?"

I had heard about Stuart Deming from the other girls. He was a student at Trinity College in Hartford, where Tom also went to school. He was considered somewhat daring and reckless, and it was rumored that he and his family had been involved in the Underground Railroad in Farmington. All I noticed were his startling blue eyes and mischievous grin.

"Good evening, Miss Allen," he said. "Would you do me the honor of sharing this dance with me?"

I was shocked. I was sure he was speaking to the wrong cousin. But as I turned my head, I could see Matty walking onto the dance floor with Tom Godard.

"I would be delighted," I replied.

CHAPTER SEVEN

Matty's Secret

"You're what?" It was not a question, but an involuntary response. I stared at what I could see of Matty's face through the darkness of our barn. So this was the big surprise, the news I had sworn to guard with my life. It was fantastic to even consider.

"Enlisting. Lincoln's going to issue another call for volunteers, and when he does I am signing up. I can't sit by and let this war pass me by."

"But Matty — you're a girl. They don't take women. What makes you think you can . . . They won't let you. Pa won't let you. I won't let you!"

"Neely, don't be silly. I'm not going to go as a girl. I'll sign up as Matthew Trescott."

"But, but you can't," I spluttered. "I mean, you're not a . . . you can't . . . how would you? You couldn't possibly. I mean, what about your . . . well, you don't have a beard. You don't look like a boy. You don't act like a boy. You aren't a boy! Boys are so — well, they're different!"

"I've passed as a man before. People only notice what they want to notice. I make a good man, really I do." She turned away into the darkness of an empty stall. When she stepped back a minute later she had on Samuel's old work jacket and a slouch cap pulled down over her ears.

"Well, whaddaya think?" she said in a deep gravelly voice.

I hated to admit it, but she was fairly convincing as she swaggered toward me.

"I think this is madness. What do you mean you've passed as a man before?"

"After Ma died, Henry and I were on our own a lot. The War had already started in Kansas, and it was a dangerous place, especially for young women. Henry had two choices when he went to town to get supplies — leave me behind to fend for myself or take his little 'brother' along. We could go more places as two boys."

I took a hard look at Matty. In the darkness of the barn it was difficult to see her features. Silhouetted, she resembled one of my brothers.

"But fighting — where in the world did you get such an idea? War is not a Saturday ride to town. It's dangerous."

Matty stared at me with that stubborn look of hers. "When we were children, what did we play, Neely? Dolls? No, we played real-life games. Joan of Arc. Indian fighters, like the boys. I can't believe you don't see it. We were never raised to accept limitations. The women in the Day family have a tradition! What about Great-grandma Day? Didn't she fight in the War of Independence? And Martha Day helped the men defend the town against the Indians when King Philip raided. My Ma helped defend our home in Kansas against Indians and border ruffians. This isn't about boys and girls. It's about fighting for what you believe."

"I know, but . . . "

"But nothing! The Day women were always fighters, one way or the other. Tonight you yourself almost fought with Mr. Bartlett!"

I blushed with shame at that memory. Matty continued, "Well, I want to fight for the Union. We were born to it, raised with it. My father and my brother are doing their part — and now it's my turn."

"You're not Joan of Arc! This isn't some romantic legend. Simsbury has already lost a dozen or more men — sick, missing, killed. For what? I can't bear to think of you like that. What if you're wounded? Dick Miller is back and he lost an arm at Antietam Creek trying to save his brother. This war is horrible. Our family has worked hard to keep the men at home, safe and sound. You can't do this. You just can't!"

"Now, Neely, don't cry. Nothing bad will happen to me."

After a moment, I regained my composure. I was surprised at how calm I sounded. "How could you do it? You aren't as strong as a boy. War is for menfolk."

"I have spent the last six years pioneering in Kansas. I can shoot and ride. I have worked all day in the fields beside Pa and Henry. Look at my hands. Feel my muscles. Henry says I'm as strong as he is." She took my hand in hers.

For the first time I noticed that Matty's hands were rough and her palms callused.

"I can even shoot better than Pa. I can reload faster than anyone on Blue Creek. I can do this Neely, really I can."

"But the danger! What if . . . "

"I know the danger, Neely, believe me. I've seen the war in Kansas. I practically grew up with it. My neighbor's boy, Jimmy Bascom, died with his head in my lap — shot in the back the night our farm was burned. There comes a time when you have to take a stand. I saw that tonight when Mr. Bartlett was talking about Isaiah. I saw the fire in your eyes at that, Neely. I heard the passion in your Pa's voice, too. There are things worth fighting for. For you it's Isaiah. For me, it's all the Isaiahs, and all the Jimmy Bascoms."

"But other things happened tonight too, Matty! What about Tom Godard? I saw *your* eyes when you danced with him! What about courtship and marriage?"

Matty smiled wistfully, carefully lowering herself onto a pile of hay. I sat down beside her.

"Yes, Tom is handsome and kind and would make a good husband. If I stayed here in Simsbury, I'm sure you and your Ma would see to it that I was engaged to him by next Christmas."

"But I still . . . "

"Don't you see? Doing what you all expect of me would be so easy, but I would miss the greatest adventure of my life! And I would be backing down from what's right!"

"Well, I can't believe I'm hearing this, but I know you, Matty Trescott. If you are determined to become a soldier, I won't be able to stop you. Still, it seems impossible."

"Nothing is impossible, Neely. You've told me so at least a hundred times. I thought we might never see each other again, and you said I was wrong. You've dreamed of going off to get a good education in Hartford, and before long you will be. You must believe in me too, Neely. I can only do this with your blessing."

"My blessing! Matty, you must be crazy! Why, I couldn't! And talk of Hartford — what are you going to say to Ma and Pa? Pa has already sent in the tuition money for the spring. He will never consent to this. Have you really thought about this?"

"I've thought about it and nothing else for days. In the first place, we aren't going to tell anyone about what I'm going to do. We will go off to Hartford together to start the spring term at the Seminary, except that only one of us is actually going to enroll."

"You mean . . . "

"Exactly, Neely."

CHAPTER EIGHT

The War Comes Closer

I've always found it strange that when I really want something to come, the time seems to drag, but when the special event arrives, I don't feel ready. Christmas and my birthday have always snuck up on me like that, and so it was that winter getting ready to leave for Hartford.

For two weeks we had been preparing all the clothes that Matty and I would need for the next five months, deciding what was necessary and what we could do without. Our small trunks didn't seem large enough to hold everything that I wanted. That last morning in my room found us doing the final packing.

"No, you'll have to leave some of your books. There just isn't room, Cornelia."

"Your mother's right, Neely," Matty teased as she walked into my room and flopped on the bed. "They do have books in Hartford you know."

"Matilda Trescott, such an unladylike pose! If you learn anything in that seminary, I hope it is proper manners!" Ma bristled. "Promise me that you will try to act appropriately when you are gone from this house."

"Oh, I promise, I promise, Aunt Phoebe. I will be a completely different person after I leave. I bet you wouldn't even know me in a few weeks time." Matty was so good at playing a scene for humor. I glared at her but she didn't blink an eye.

"Yes, dear, I'm sure you will *try*. But remember, you've been mostly around men out there in Kansas. Hartford society is much more refined. Do keep your mother in mind while you are at the Seminary. She had such high hopes for you and your brother. It would have broken her heart to see the family broken up and your brother and father off fighting in the army. Please try to follow Neely's good example while you are in Hartford."

"I will, I really will. Every minute I am there." She sounded so sincere I almost believed her. The truth is that she did not intend to stay in Hartford any longer than she had to.

Later in the day Pa came back from the Post Office,

looking grim. He had a copy of the Hartford *Courant* in his hands.

"What is it, Pa? What is it? Bad news about the War?"

"The War is coming too close to home, Neely. There has been an explosion in Hartford, at Colt's factory where they make firearms and repeating pistols. Some think it was deliberately done, by Confederates or southern sympathizers. Truth is no one knows what happened. I'm not sure how Ma will take this news with you and Matty leaving for Hartford tomorrow." He shook his head.

I stood staring at him, his large frame filling the kitchen, his gentle face taken over by a look I had never seen before. My father had always seemed a gentle giant of a man, unflappable and steady. He had never appeared afraid or upset about anything. I pondered what he'd said about Ma and thought maybe he was trying to tell me that *he* was afraid for me, that *he* wasn't sure that I should go.

"Pa, Ma will take it all right. If this is the act of raiders, then we are in just as much danger here in Simsbury, with the Toy-Bickford fuse factory practically in the center of town. No one would want to destroy the Seminary, and besides, the War is almost over, isn't it? Matty says that General Grant will take it to Robert E. Lee pretty quickly and if Lee is finally beaten, the War will end. Won't it?"

"Could be, sweetie, could be. Let's not tell your Ma the news till after supper."

"Okay, Pa. I can keep a secret if you can."

It turned out Ma was not that upset about the happenings in Hartford, and never said a word about our not going. The Allen that took the Colt fire the hardest was my brother Jonathan. That night he came to my room and sat on the corner of my bed. I thought he had come to say good-bye. I was right, sort of.

"You're what? You can't be serious!" This couldn't be happening again!

"Enlisting. Joining up to fight those rebels. Lincoln is calling for volunteers and the bonus is more than we made last year on the entire corn crop. If Pa and Samuel don't see their duty, that's their business, but this War is something I can't avoid."

"Ma won't let you, and Pa would never give his consent. Not in a million years. Besides, you're too young. They don't take boys your age, you know."

"I am going to pretend to be older. I can do it. I heard tell that if you put a piece of paper in your shoe with the number eighteen on it, then you can swear that you are 'over eighteen' and not be lying. Other guys have done it. Henry Burr is a corporal in his unit and he isn't much older than I am."

"Henry Burr is a fool who broke his mother's heart by running off in the dead of night. Besides, he was wounded at Antietam Creek. And lots of men from Simsbury have died in the War. You aren't going — I won't allow it."

"Oh, you're just as bad as Samuel. I agree with Matty. A real man has to stand up for what he believes."

At the mention of Matty, a plot hatched in my mind. I saw a way to solve two problems at once.

"Matty, of course. Matty. Why don't we go talk to her about this? Maybe she can convince you of your folly."

My confidence was growing. Hearing these ideas from Jonathan would make her see how foolish it all was.

"Let's go find her now," I said. "I think she is upstairs writing to her Pa."

As we entered the room, Jonathan anxiously pushed ahead of me. He deposited his lanky frame in the rocker by the nightstand and stared intently at Matty. Her letter writing interrupted, Matty looked up, giving me a grin. I jerked my head toward Jonathan and grimaced.

"Rather a strange way to enter milady's chamber, Master Allen," she chirped, affecting an English accent. "To what do I owe the honor? Come to say good-bye, I suppose, or to pledge undying love?" But this always reliable game did not produce the desired effect.

"Neely doesn't understand, but I told her you would. She is so insulated here in Simsbury, not up on war news and the like. Tell her I am old enough. Tell her how important it is for me to do my part. You know how it is. You've seen this war up close. Tell her."

"Tell her *what*? What is it she needs to hear from me?"

Matty's voice was slow and deliberate. She glanced questioningly at me.

"He wants you to tell me why he should run away and enlist in the army. Disguise himself and pretend to be old enough to fight. Sneak off in the middle of the night without telling anyone. He thinks you'll approve." I tried to keep my voice even, but I think a judgmental tone slipped out. I did not care.

Matty's eyes opened wide and her brow wrinkled. A look of panic flashed in her eyes and I knew the wheels in her brain were turning rapidly. I almost smiled at her predicament.

"No one else in this house understands, Matty. No one but you feels like I do. Your pa and brother are lucky to be fighting those damn rebels. Mr. Lincoln has called for new volunteers and I am going. I'd almost decided before, but the news about the Colt factory made my mind up. Those damned Confederates and their copperhead cowardly — "

"Jonathan, keep your voice down and watch your language. Do you want Ma to hear you swearing like that?" I couldn't believe I was taking him to task for his rough words when the matter at hand was much more serious. Life is funny sometimes.

"Sorry, Neely. I just get so mad that I . . . I . . . well, I don't know what to do. At least I didn't, but now I do. I have to do this. I just have to." He looked pleadingly at Matty, who was still recovering from the shock. I was sure I had her. After a second she spoke.

"I know the feeling, Jonathan. It's a pushing sensation in your chest and in your brain that never goes away and never lets up. You feel like you'll never be right again until you do something about it. I know that well."

This wasn't going the way I'd hoped. Still I couldn't imagine that Matty would encourage him to go. Jonathan leaned forward eagerly. I gave Matty a panicked look.

"And I think you would make a fine soldier," she continued. "We need fine young men in the army fighting for what they think is right. I admire your spirit and I admire your courage. We had that kind of courage at Gettysburg."

"But — " I interrupted in desperation.

"But that is not the question, is it? You want to know if I think you should enlist. It sounds farfetched, doesn't it? A boy of your age has much to overcome. You are tall enough to be a soldier, but long legs are no substitute for muscles. Besides, your voice still squeaks at times." Jonathan started to protest, but Matty's gently raised hand silenced him.

"Now don't be offended. I am not saying that you couldn't be a good soldier. I am saying that it would be hard to pull off, that's all. You would have as much trouble convincing someone you were a man as Neely would. And you cannot run off and break your mother's heart. This family needs you at home to help run the farm. With

Samuel off at Yale and Neely in Hartford, both of your parents will be needing you more than ever."

"But what about the War? We can't just let the Confederates get away with bringing the War to Hartford, can we? Don't we have to stand up and fight?" His eyes were filling with tears and I began to feel that I might cry too.

"Bobby Lee will soon be beaten with or without you, Jonathan," she answered.

"It's for the best, Jonny," I said, patting his hand. "Let's sleep on this. I am sure it will look different in the morning." He smiled weakly.

"Neely's right. A night's sleep will do us all some good," Matty chimed in.

"You won't tell anyone about this, will you? I mean, I promise not to do anything right away, but I still might when I am older."

"Yes, when you are my age you might get away with it," Matty said. She glanced calmly at me. I knew she hadn't changed her mind.

CHAPTER NINE

Off to Hartford!

"Oh, Matty, can you believe it? We are off to Hartford at last! Oh, I can't bear it — see how sad Ma looks." I peered through the dirty window of the train at my family standing on the wooden platform. Jonathan stood off to the side, smiling bravely. We had just settled into our hard seats, and I was arranging my petticoats when I saw Benjamin gesturing frantically. "Oh look, wave to Benjamin! I can't believe we're actually leaving Simsbury."

"We'll be in Plainville in about an hour, Neely. After we change trains there, we'll be in Hartford before you know it." Matty was in such good spirits, as if a huge weight had been lifted from her shoulders.

As the little train moved southward out of the station, I felt strange: on one hand, very grown-up and free, setting off to find my way in the world — my adventure, as Matty would say. At the same time, I felt a terrible sadness, loneliness really, leaving behind my home and family, all the things I was sure about in the world, to head for something unknown. What made it worse was that everyone assumed my leaving would be easier with Matty's accompanying me. The burden of her secret made my loneliness greater.

I was also afraid, yet still hopeful that Matty would change her mind at the last minute. There seemed to be so many problems with her plan, and I did not believe she could pull off her masquerade as a man. I had told her so a few nights before we left.

"Oh, you worry too much," she had replied. "That is the least of our problems."

I didn't dare ask what other problems she meant.

We had spent a lot of time working out the story I was to tell the teachers at the Seminary, as well as the Battersons, the family in Hartford with whom I was going to board. In my bag was a note Matty had written on Pa's stationery informing Mr. Crosby, principal of the Seminary, that "due to certain changes in plans" young Matilda Trescott would not be attending the Seminary during the spring semester, and the school was to retain the extra money and apply it to my tuition in the fall. Another note for Mrs. Batterson requested that a similar arrangement be made with the money for Matty's room and board.

But the worst part of the plan was the lying I would have to do, especially to Ma and Pa. Not a day had passed since the Phelps' party that I did not raise this objection to my obstinate cousin.

"You can be such a mouse sometimes, Neely," she had retorted. "I'm the one who is going to have it hard — living in a tent, marching and fighting. Eating cold food. You shall be safe and warm, well-fed, washed and combed, and carefree. Learning all the wonders in your books. Besides, I'm going to arrange to have my bonus money and half my pay sent to you, so you'll be rich as well."

When she started talking like that, there was nothing I could say. She actually succeeded in making me feel bad that I was complaining about my problems. Besides, I knew Matty, knew she would go no matter what I said. Most of the time, I thought only about what it would be like waiting for her letters, wondering if she were alive or dead. I decided I was not afraid of what Ma and Pa would say when they found out I had lied to them, but I was petrified about what they would say if Matty were wounded or killed in battle. Her death was more than I could bear to think about, so I struggled to keep such ideas out of my head.

Changing trains in Plainville was easy. We had just gotten off the southbound Canal Railroad train when the eastbound Hartford and Providence train came chugging into the station. I worried that our luggage would not be shifted in time, but not Matty. She had such confidence in the arrangements, the whole plan really, that she could not imagine that the railroads could ruin it for us. Besides, all the clothes she would need were packed in a small duffel bag she held tightly. The clothes, I must add, that she had stolen from Samuel as her final joke — her revenge for his eternal teasing!

The little train chugged out of Plainville, a smoky trail marking its passage. As the cloud dispersed, I felt my fear and doubt disappearing with it. I began to feel excited about starting at the Seminary. We rode in silence for a long while. Outside, the brightness of the winter sun was broken only by the bare trees speeding by.

"Matty, we are on the last leg of our — my trip. Hartford is the next stop!"

"I know. I'm glad for you. You are going to be a real lady, educated and genteel, with the freedom to do whatever you want. I know that these last few weeks have been difficult and I know that I have been a little bossy . . . "

"A little?"

"Well, then, a lot. But our plan works only if we make no mistakes. I just — well, never mind. I want you to succeed at the Seminary, like we both know you can, and not worry about me."

"You know that's impossible. All the years you were in Kansas we wrote regularly, and you were never far from my thoughts. We're more than cousins, Matty — we're sisters. Your danger is my own. Your hopes and dreams are mine. That's why I can let you go, but it's also why you can't tell me not to worry."

She smiled. "Look, we're pulling into Hartford. Now, you have the letters and you know what to say. If anyone asks you any questions you don't want to answer, just change the subject, or act stupid like Cousin Sarah. You know how she is, kind of helpless and brainless? Anyway, the school will be sending a carriage for you and I will make sure they've come before I leave." She leaned over and kissed my cheek. "You're my best friend, Neely, and my sister. I love you — never forget that."

Before I could speak, the train came jerking to a halt. Matty jumped up, grabbed my hand, and pulled me up the aisle and down the steps to the platform. As we were jostled by the crowd, I suddenly remembered that I had no idea which unit she was planning to join. I called to her to slow down and tried to ask her, but at that moment I heard a voice behind me.

"Miss Allen? Miss Cornelia Allen? I am Mr. Martin, of the Hartford Female Seminary. I have a coach waiting for you. Shall we find your baggage?"

In a flash, Matty whirled and spoke. "Yes, this is Miss Allen. I believe her trunks are over there." I noticed that she had said "trunks," referring to hers along with mine. She really was going to leave me!

"Ah," said Mr. Martin, "and are you her cousin, Miss Trescott?"

"Oh no, I am just an acquaintance of the family, on my way to visit my poor aunt in Meriden." Looking at me, she said, "So nice to see you again, Miss Allen. Do keep in touch."

With that, she turned and disappeared into the crowd.

CHAPTER TEN

Stony Mountain

My Dearest Cousin, *February 25, 1864*

You must forgive my tardiness in writing, but I have been so busy and so tired that only now am I finding time and energy to write to you. As you can imagine, they keep us pretty busy.

Let me start at the beginning. After I left you, I caught the late train for New Haven, arriving there after dark. I decided to use part of my spending money to secure a hotel room, and spent the night in style. I got the room mostly to have a safe place to change my clothes, but found I was glad to have some time to myself, as it was hard to say good-bye to the Matilda part of me. I gave a false name when I checked in, and told the clerk I was from Ohio. I also told him that my brother was calling for me in the morning, to avert suspicion if anyone were to see me leaving as Matthew.

The next morning I cut my hair, changed into the clothes I'd stolen from Samuel, and packed my Matilda clothes. I had to get rid of all traces of my old self, and resolved to throw my girl's clothing into the ocean. I took some hotel stationery and wrote a letter giving my address as Baltimore, Maryland, and put it in the bag so anyone who found it would not trace it to me. I left early to avoid being seen, and took a long walk down by the wharf. When no one was looking, I tossed the bag into the harbor, said a brief farewell to Matilda, and set off to find some breakfast.

After eating, I found my way to the armory where several hundred men milled around waiting for the place to open. Although I was apprehensive, enlisting was easier than you might have thought. I was asked to sign a paper swearing that I was over eighteen and that I was not a deserter, a mental defective, or a criminal. The worst part was the waiting, but I heard that it was good practice, as the army spends most of its time waiting for something.

We were sworn in and issued uniforms and blankets, courtesy of the ladies of New Haven. I was not sure how I would get my uniform on without being found out. As I stood waiting for inspiration, I noticed that several of the lads were putting their uniforms on over their regular clothes. I did the same. I was lucky that it was February and very cold.

We spent the afternoon waiting. I kept to myself, sitting in the corner listening to the others swapping stories and rumors. Eventually we were marched over to the train station. The New Haven ladies were again out in force, this time with kettles of soup, and crackers, corn bread, and hot coffee. We boarded the train laden with hot food and hospitality, thanks to the fair ladies of that fair city.

We left New Haven Wednesday evening and had a long, cold train ride, arriving at Washington City early Friday morning. I would have liked to sightsee a little, but of course we were not given any time for such things, and instead had to march from the station over to Camp Wright without any breakfast. As tired and hungry as I was, it was stirring to be marching through the streets of this most famous of cities.

We did get to see something of the city along the way, and it was exciting to catch sight of the newly completed dome on the Capitol building. It was so large and impressive and made my heart swell with pride. The other interesting sight was a half-

finished granite monument, which someone said was to be a memorial to George Washington. It was very impressive, soaring over one hundred feet toward the sky, and stood just to the west of the Capitol building. I felt like a tourist, standing before it in the cold and sleet.

Camp Wright was just a training base, about three miles from the city. It was supposed to house over ten thousand new soldiers at one time, and I could believe that, as white tents stretched for miles in every direction. More than men, it seemed that every horse and mule in all of creation were there. One drive came in with over seven thousand mules.

Life there was confusing. They made us drill constantly, and we had to march everywhere and wait for hours every time we arrived at our destination. Here we were issued our gear, including a new Connecticut-made Sharp's rifle. Having my rifle made me itchy for a fight.

We were only at Camp Wright for a few days before being shipped south to meet up with the Fourteenth Regiment. Our train went to Brandy Station, fifty miles southwest, a trip that took fourteen hours, since there were thousands of soldiers and civilians riding back and forth daily. We arrived on Washington's birthday, which I took as a good sign, though no one else seemed to. We were hungry and tired but had to be welcomed by the officers and listen to a number of speeches before we were allowed to join our units. I was so tired that I ate a little cold supper and lay down on the frozen ground and slept without any blanket. The veterans in my unit say that being hungry is good practice for battle.

We are camped a few miles south of Brandy Station, in an area called Stony Mountain. We are not ignoring the enemy, you can be sure. They are camped a few miles south of us, just the other side of the Rapidan River, and we do have to keep a careful watch. Every other week our regiment pulls guard duty and then each company supplies two sentries. Soon it will be my turn.

For now, there is another favor I must ask. In my trunk, hidden behind the lining in the back, you will find a number of letters written to my Pa and Henry, and five dollars to cover the postage. I need you to mail one regularly, as Pa and Henry will worry if they don't hear from me once in a while. These are simple letters, filled with endless chatter about the boring life of the Seminary and how much I wish I could be with them. I hope this will satisfy them for a while.

Neely, there is still one more secret you must keep. The night before we left the farm, I buried something very dear to me under the rock by the old apple tree. You know which tree I mean – on the hill where we used to play pirates. I think it is well hidden and safe there. But if I should not return from this war, I want you to have it, a final gift from

Your loving cousin,

Matt

CHAPTER ELEVEN

At the Seminary

"Neely! Hurry or you'll be late for drawing class," called my friend Mary. "What is that letter you're reading?"

Hastily I put Matty's letter into my sketch pad and changed the subject. It wasn't hard to distract Mary with a joke about the drawing instructor, who had an affected way of talking that he no doubt considered very "cultured."

I was, of course, sick with worry about Matty and filled with remorse about having lied to Ma and Pa about her. I yearned to share my worries with someone, but I'd sworn to Matty that I would keep her secret, so I had to remain silent. Soon life at the Seminary became so full of things to do and learn that some days, I must confess, I would go for hours without thinking about her.

Because I had been a good student at the district school, I was placed directly in the "second division" of the Seminary. To my delight, I was quick at Latin, and quite advanced in natural history owing to my years on the farm. I had always been intrigued by nature and was thrilled that it was a respectable school subject. The other courses at the Seminary promised to be very interesting. We learned things like higher arithmetic, as well as English and history. These were the same subjects my brother Samuel was studying at Yale, so I would be his equal in the sciences and mathematics — perhaps I would be even better!

Catharine Beecher, who had founded the Seminary, wasn't there any more, but our teachers tried to help us learn according to her principles. At the district school in Simsbury, I got along on just my memory, but the Seminary required more thinking. "Reason it out!" Miss Goldthwaite would tell us. She had been there for more than fifteen years, but many of our teachers were younger, like Miss Barry and Miss Palmer. In addition to our regular teachers, professors from the men's colleges nearby came to deliver lectures. I was looking forward to hearing the famous chemist, Benjamin Silliman of Yale, and the geologist Edward Hitchcock from Amherst College in Massachusetts.

The Seminary was located on Pratt Street in Hartford,

and I lived just a few blocks away with the Battersons, whose daughter Clara also attended the school. Clara wasn't a very good student, but she was fun-loving and kind. Some of my more distant cousins — Annie Allen from Hartford and Julia Day from West Avon — were also classmates, but fortunately they hadn't heard that Matty was supposed to be at the Seminary, so her absence didn't cause any problems. Girls from all around the country attended the Seminary, including three sisters — Alice, Eva, and Josephine Eldridge — from Lawrence, Kansas. Their father and brothers, like Matty's, were at war. Making friends with girls from faraway places like New York City, Wisconsin, and Ohio was easy, because they were lonely for their families too. But the Hartford girls were more clannish and harder to get to know, except those like Clara who had classmates living with them.

My best friend was Mary Talcott, who came from New Britain and had a fine humorous bent. Mary was forever cutting poems and articles out of the newspaper and showing them to me. One of her favorites was a mocking "national anthem of the South":

> O say, can you see — though perhaps you're too tight
> What so feebly we hailed at the twilight's last beaming
> Whose broad bars and few stars o'er our scurrilous flight
> From the rumshops we filched, were so gaudily streaming?
> When the rockets' red glare and bombs bursting in air
> Gave proof that, though we ran, our rag remained there!

O, say, does that Bar-Strangled Banner still wave
O'er the land of the thief and the home of the slave?

Yes, Mary made me laugh and my teachers made me think. Yet at the back of my mind, I could not forget that in mid-April the principals, Mr. and Mrs. Crosby, would be sending home to each girl's parents a report on our attendance and scholarly achievements. What would happen when Ma and Pa got a report about me but none about Matty?

CHAPTER TWELVE

Brandy Station

My Dearest Cousin, *March 28, 1864*

I must apologize for my slowness in writing. Part of the problem is, of course, the army work schedule, but aside from that, I have been making some friends here and have been busy after hours as well. It took a third letter from you to remind me how long it has been since I last wrote.

Life in camp has quickly become routine. We are assigned tents, although many of the men have built lean-tos or shacks. I share a tent with Private Dick Slocum. He is a nice boy, rather quiet and shy, which is fine with me because he is always sneaking off to be by himself to change his clothes or to use the latrine in private, and so I have more privacy. He is from Putnam, way up in the eastern corner of the state. Like me, he is a new recruit, untried and untested. He seems even more nervous than I am, but surely that is because he is so young. Also, I think he is homesick, as I have heard him crying in his sleep. I feel sorry for him – I know how hard it is to be away from family for the first time.

Two weeks after I arrived we were ordered back to Brandy Station to provide extra troops for support, as General Grant was coming in to assume command of the army. It was a miserable day, raining and cold, and I stood in the pouring rain for six hours and never got a glimpse of the General. I am beginning to see that this is what war, or the army, is all about: waiting and watching, and being cold, wet, and miserable.

My unit is the Fourteenth Connecticut Volunteer Infantry Regiment. It was originally formed in the summer of 1862 and was over seventeen hundred strong before its first service at the Union victory at Antietam in Maryland, in September of 1862. The Fourteenth served bravely in the defeats at Fredericksburg and Chancellorsville. They received special commendations from General Hancock for repelling the charge by General Pickett at Gettysburg.

We are not fighting right now, as the army is in winter quarters. Since the beginning of time, armies have rested up in winter: It is too hard to move and fight in snow and ice, and even harder to pitch tents in frozen ground. Around here it is said that the Romans named the month of March after their war god Mars because that was traditionally the beginning of the warring season. If that is true, then every sign of spring is a reminder that we will face the enemy very soon.

In order to pass the time, we devise numerous amusements. Some play games, like baseball and football, while others organize foot races and gymnastic events. I prefer quieter games, such as quoits and horseshoes, and enjoy the nightly singing around the campfires. At first, I was careful not to sing too loud as my voice is much too high, but I have found that several of the young men have voices like mine or higher, so now I sing as the spirit moves me.

I am amazed at how well I have settled into army life. Although I hate to admit it, initially I wasn't sure that I would be able to pull it off, but now I find that my new identity has become so natural to me that I seldom have to think about it. There are, of course, certain problems with being the only girl (that I know of!) among several thousand men.

The most pressing problem is using the latrine, but here in winter camp it is not too difficult to find some privacy. On cold days, most of the men stay inside the little huts they have built, and on warm days many go off into the woods looking for firewood or hunting squirrels and rabbits. Either way, I can usually find a private place, and when necessary, I wait until after dark.

Another problem is bathing. The real issue here is not privacy but facilities. Living outside in the winter with no bathtub or kettles for boiling enough water to wash properly is the main drawback, so nearly everyone washes up in his tent or hut. A few brave souls do find the courage to bathe in the river, but I would not do that in this cold weather even if I were a man.

As I told you, I thought I might have to bind my breasts to make them less noticeable, but I found that wearing several layers of clothing made this unnecessary. I am not sure what the warmer weather will bring, but I think it may not be a problem even then as my uniform is made of coarse stiff wool. The real problem will be wearing hot itchy wool in July. As for my other female "peculiarity," this seems to have taken care of itself, as I haven't had to deal with it for a few months. Ma once told me that strenuous work and little food could cause it to disappear for a while, and I guess she was right. I am glad, as this could have been a serious problem. I just hope it doesn't come back to haunt me in battle.

Last week we were hit by a blizzard, and some of the men organized a huge snowball fight. It lasted all day and into the evening, with my side building a snow fort and then charging the other side's position. We even took prisoners. Here we were, serious soldiers waiting for the real thing, playing at mock war. Later that night, two of my new friends, Petey Wilson and Irv Stoneman, "found" several chickens and cooked up a stew for the entire company. They are very resourceful, and nice boys besides. After we ate, we played cards and told stories until almost midnight. This was fun, but it made me homesick, and it was hard for me not to talk about Simsbury or Kansas.

I have told everyone that I am from the Nebraska Territory and that when my parents died, I returned east to find my grandparents. After searching for three months, I ran out of money and decided to join up and fight for the Union. This is a good story as I don't imagine I'll find anyone else in the regiment from out West. It also allows me to talk with the boys about farm life and life on the frontier, since they are all interested in conditions in the territories and never tire of asking me questions.

Since last week's snows, the spring winds have been drying the ground, and we all know what that means. General Grant is planning our first move, assuming that General Lee doesn't outfox him and move first. Some of the men think that Lee cannot hold out much longer, that our superior numbers will sooner or later make the difference, but others believe that all our generals are incompetent. These last men are saying that soon we will be taking our annual beating at Bull Run, but I think they are wrong. General Grant is a wonderful leader, with a solid string of victories in the west. He turned defeat into victory at Shiloh, was successful in his siege at Vicksburg last summer, and worked wonders at the battles for Chattanooga. Still, the doubters say he hasn't faced Bobby Lee yet, but I say that Bobby Lee hasn't faced U. S. Grant yet. Only time will tell.

My company, Company G, has had sentry duty three times since I got here and I have had duty each time, even though there are twenty-nine men besides me. But that is all part of being the new "man," and I take my turn gladly. These brave men have proven their courage in battle, and I must endure whatever initiation it takes for them to learn to trust me. It is only fair.

I talk about the men as if I am one of them, and although I am keeping a huge secret from them all, I do feel that I am "one of the boys." There is a big Irishman here named O'Rourke, who teases me about having such a baby face and not needing to shave. He's given me the nickname "Molly," but this is good-natured and I do not mind. Each time I hear it, I laugh to myself

CHAPTER THIRTEEN

A Letter from Home

The late April rain pelted the sidewalks of Hartford as I hurried through the streets on my way back to the Battersons' house. Just as I feared, there was a letter from Ma.

Under ordinary circumstances, I would have been happy to hear news of my family. But mid-semester grades had been sent home recently, and I knew the arrival of the grades would lead to trouble. My hands trembled as I opened the envelope.

Dearest Neely,

We are so proud of you! You have done so very well at the Seminary this first term. It has confirmed for your father and me how right we were to send you to Hartford to further your education.

Of course, the Day women were always smart! Look at your great-aunt Mary, one of the first to go to the Normal School in New Britain. And of course, Rachel and I both did well at school although our schooling never went as far as Mary's.

Speaking of Day women, how is Matty doing? We haven't heard from her in a long time (of course, that's the Trescott in her – they never were much at letter writing!). For some reason, we did not receive Matty's mid-semester report from the Crosbys. Would you please look into this? Perhaps it was sent to Kansas by mistake.

All is well on the farm. With the coming of spring, we are all very busy and there is much to do! But it is so beautiful that I don't mind being so busy.

Jonathan gets a little taller every day and Benjamin is continually into trouble. Samuel's studies at Yale seem to be going well, though not so well as his sister's!

Your father and I send our love to you. And to Matty too, of course.

Your loving
Mother

I couldn't believe it! I had feared my world would crumble at my feet when Ma and Pa didn't receive Matty's mid-semester report. But instead, Ma simply attributed it to a mistake on the part of the Crosbys. Or maybe just to Matty being a Trescott! ("You know those Trescotts — they never were any good at getting their grades mailed home!") Bless Ma and her opinions!

I did a little dance for joy. This meant they wouldn't find out the truth for a little while longer. I reached in the drawer and pulled out a fresh sheet of writing paper. I wanted to put Ma's questions to rest as soon as possible.

My joy didn't last long. Soon I was overtaken by the guilt of lying to Ma and Pa, who were always so good to me. How could I keep on deceiving them? I was such an undeserving daughter! How would I ever make it up to them? What would the summer be like when I had to go home and face up to my lies?

I threw myself into my studies, thinking perhaps if I studied hard enough, the guilt would go away. Or perhaps I wouldn't notice it as much. But all the Latin verbs and botanical terms that filled my head couldn't drown out the cries of a guilty conscience.

CHAPTER FOURTEEN

Brandy Station

My dearest Cousin, *April 25, 1864*

So much has happened since I last wrote that I hardly know where to begin. I guess until now you have not known if I was alive or dead, so the first news is the most obvious: I'm alive and kicking! But not bragging, perhaps.

I cannot tell you how much I enjoyed the package you sent me. The cookies and fudge were delicious, even though a little dried out from their trip. I shared them with my bunkmate Dickey, and with Wilson and Stoneman, and each one offered you a marriage proposal for your kindness. Wilson and Stoneman are too old for you, but Dick would be a good match. He is sensitive and observant and interested in nature. I have been talking about you and he said if you wouldn't mind, he would like to write to you. I know it would mean a lot to him. He's lonely and hasn't made many friends here.

As for the letters from Pa and Henry, I had not thought about how to handle these and am glad you were able to send them along. They are more precious than gold and I have read each one a dozen times. I only hope it did not cause you to tell too many lies to provide me with such treasures. I am including a few letters I have written to them, answering their questions about the Seminary, at least as much as I know after reading your letters.

Some good news: My friend Brian O'Rourke was promoted to corporal. I have heard that he is fearless in battle and was responsible for saving many lives in the failed charge at Fredericksburg. Even though he continues to tease me, he is a real friend. I'm beginning to see that friendship is so important here in the army. It is a good feeling to know that when my life depends on others, these men will stand beside me.

The last time I wrote we were getting ready for a brigade review by Colonel Carroll on the 14th of April. It was a lot of work but well worth it. We had to wait over an hour in full parade uniform, but it was a cool day, and it was a joyous occasion when the Colonel rode by. He stopped and talked to the Captain and had high praise for the Fourteenth. The veterans made light of Colonel Carroll's remarks, but the truth is, there wasn't a man in the regiment who did swell with pride at the Colonel's comments.

The next day we had a full division review over at Stevensburg. We got up very early and marched for over an hour to get there. We arrived a dusty and sorry-looking lot. But I did not care. It was a splendid affair, which I was thrilled to be a part of. It was cloudy and threatened rain all morning, but the army isn't cowed by a little weather. The highlight of the day was seeing General Hancock as he rode by. He is a handsome man and he looked dashing in the saddle. I found myself thinking of his wife, wondering if she had ever seen him in such splendor. If I ever marry, it will be to a splendid warrior like that. Not to some young doctor that you would have me marry. It seems odd to write this to you as I make every effort to think and act like a man, but every so often I find these thoughts creeping out. I guess you cannot suppress Nature. Perhaps you could find reasons for this in your studies.

As if the review were not enough to excite us to march to Richmond and hang all the rebels at midnight, a few days later we had a corps review, presided over by none other than General

U. S. Grant himself! I would like to report to you that I got a good look at our great leader, but the truth is I was lost in a sea of blue caps and managed only to catch a brief glimpse of what I think was his horse's tail. Not much to brag about, but it is a start. As a lowly private, I know I cannot hope to meet him, but I do hope I will have other opportunities at least to see him from afar.

With the seriousness of military inspections behind us, we have returned to our lazy life. This is made easier by the warmer, longer days, but the signs of spring only remind us that the easy routine of winter is fleeting. Each day we know we are one step closer to the real thing.

Don't worry so much about me, Neely dear. If I do go into battle, I shall be all right. I don't believe there are any Rebel bullets made for me yet.

Your loving cousin,
Matt

CHAPTER FIFTEEN

Cousins Come to Call

Early May brought a profusion of flowers to Hartford's gardens, and the Battersons' yard was no exception. With a weekend assignment to collect flowers for natural history class, I spent Saturday afternoon gathering flowers with Clara Batterson outside her home.

"Oh, isn't this one beautiful!" exclaimed Clara, waving a vivid pink peony in the air.

"But we already have some peonies," I protested.

"Yes, but this one is prettier."

"Clara," I said patiently, "this is about gathering different *forms* of flowers, not different colors of the same flower."

Clara sniffed. "I still don't see why we can't just pick whatever we want. Flowers are flowers, aren't they?"

I started to explain the need to study nature scientifically but was interrupted by the sound of familiar voices in the front yard.

"Clara!" I exclaimed, trying to keep my voice to a whisper. "That sounds just like my cousin Ira and his son Wallace! What could they be doing here? Shhhhhh! Let's listen and not let them know we're out here."

Clara and I hid behind a tall hedge that separated the side yard from the front of the house. My cousins had stopped to talk by the front gate.

"Now, remember to tell Cornelia how well she looks," I heard Cousin Ira say. "Young ladies like that sort of thing."

"Yes, yes, Pa," came Wallace's squeaky voice, sounding impatient. "But you know she already adores me!"

What? How had Wallace ever concocted such an idea? I could feel myself blush with fury and embarrassment. Clara giggled. I was afraid she would give away our hiding place if I didn't find an excuse to send her inside.

"Sshhhhhh! Clara, go put these flowers inside in some water before they die," I whispered, gesturing to indicate that she should go to the back of the house. Reluctantly, Clara did as I asked.

"Ladies with light hair and pale eyes aren't my favorites though," Wallace was telling his father. "I like the dark ones with flashing eyes like Matilda."

Matty! Of course, they would expect to see Matty too. What was I to do? Somehow I had to keep Ira and Wallace from speaking to the Battersons, or even entering their house. I could make up some excuse for Matty's absence — that was easy. But if Clara or her mother were to talk to my cousins, I would have a lot of explaining to do.

Taking a deep breath, I stepped through the hedge, a welcoming smile pasted on my face.

"Cousin Ira! Cousin Wallace! How lovely to see you! What are you doing in Hartford?"

Ira took a step backward, clearly startled. "Cornelia!" he exclaimed. "What a very strange way to greet your guests!"

"Father and I are in town on business," smirked Wallace patronizingly. "And your ma asked us to drop off a package for you."

"How sweet of you to visit!" I simpered, lowering my eyes in what I hoped was a properly ladylike manner. I wasn't used to acting this way.

"Yes, we're in town to purchase merchandise for the Allen store. We're expanding, you know," continued Ira self-importantly. "Otherwise we wouldn't be here. Don't much like the city. Too crowded, too noisy."

"And too dusty. Aren't you going to invite us in?" asked Wallace.

I gulped. I could see Clara at the front window, peering through the curtains. "It's so lovely out here!" I exclaimed, taking Wallace's arm. I opened my "pale eyes" wide and gave him a look that he could interpret as adoring. "Why don't we just stroll around the gardens?"

"Should we ask Matty to join us?" asked Cousin Ira.

"She's a trifle indisposed, I regret to say." I looked down, trying to convey the idea that it was some "feminine problem" so that they wouldn't inquire further. "She'll be so sorry that she missed you both! But I'll convey your warm regards to her."

Wallace looked disappointed. "Well, here's your package. Your ma thought you could use your light summer cloak what with the weather getting so warm and all." He shoved the parcel into my arms.

"And Cousin Sarah baked you these cakes," added Ira, handing me a larger package.

"Why thank you both and send my thanks to Sarah too," I said, trying to sound grateful, and looking for a place to put the packages down. We came to a bench in the garden, and as I placed them there, I saw Clara's face, now in the kitchen window.

"I hope they are teaching *you* to bake cakes here," said Wallace.

"Why no," I said. "We are learning Latin and natural history and — "

"Foolishness!" sniffed Ira.

"What would a lady need with such learning?" asked Wallace, genuinely puzzled.

"Why should my brother Samuel learn Latin and algebra,

for that matter? And if he does, why shouldn't I? I've always been the better student!"

"Well, I always thought Sam was putting on airs, going to Yale and all," admitted Wallace. "But at least he's a man."

"Yes," agreed Ira. "I've never held with this educating young ladies. A shameful waste of money. And it makes them think they're too good to be wives and mothers."

"You don't want to end up like your great-aunt Mary Day, do you?" Wallace added. "She went to that normal school in New Britain, and now she's an old maid schoolteacher!"

My patience with my two cousins was wearing thin, but I managed another smile. "So sweet of you to worry about me and my future happiness, dear cousin," I said. I took each man's arm and, walking between them, propelled them back to the front yard.

"Well, I know you two are very busy men," I said. "I shan't detain you any longer."

"But shouldn't we pay our respects to Mrs. Batterson, while we are here?" asked Ira.

"Oh no, cousin, she's much too busy with her baking and cooking and sewing and — "

"Good woman," said Ira.

"Yes, yes, she is," I agreed hastily. "I will send your regards to her too. Now good-bye, dear cousins and thank you for the kind visit."

When at last they had gone, I gathered up my packages and hurried into the house. Waves of relief swept over me. I had passed another important test, but how many more would there be?

Clara was sitting at the parlor window, pretending to read.

"Your cousin is very tall and thin," she said, looking up. "But he might be a proper beau for — "

"Certainly not for me!" I laughed, opening my packages. "But his mother does bake excellent cakes! Want one?"

CHAPTER SIXTEEN

The Wilderness

Dearest Neely, *May 5, 1864*

The big news came on May first. We were told to tear down our huts and pitch our tents again. This was made very difficult by a severe storm that arrived in the early afternoon, causing high winds. At one point the wind was so fierce that a good-sized pine tree broke off about twenty feet above the ground and landed on Colonel Ellis's tent. Luckily the Colonel was out riding at the time and no one was injured. I was nearby digging a privy when it happened. I ducked for cover when it came crashing down. I had to laugh when I got to thinking about it afterwards, remembering my promise to you to come back safe and sound. Imagine the joke of it: killed by a falling tree before the battle had begun! While digging a privy!

We spent the next few days preparing for battle. Over the winter we had collected chairs, tables, pots, pans, books, and such items as made life a little easier. Now we had to discard them, as we had to carry everything we needed with us.

Our supply wagons carry our food, extra ammunition, and medical supplies, but each man has to carry his own gear. Just carrying a rifle, canteen, and a few extra clothes in your pack is a heavy burden when you have to march all day in the hot sun. When we took our tent down, Dick and I unbuttoned it and each of us now carries half a tent. I am stronger than Dickey, but I think he would be embarrassed if I suggested carrying his half too. To save weight and space in their packs, some men even burned their letters from home, keeping only the most recent. I considered doing this, but your letters are my only link with home and my past, with the real me. I can not bring myself to destroy your letters. They are a small burden to help me feel connected to you.

Late in the day on Tuesday, May third, messengers began to appear on horseback. By supper time our pickets, or guards, were called in, extra rations were distributed, and our ammo boxes ordered filled with sixty rounds each. After supper, word went out to extinguish all fires and maintain silence. Many of the men, anticipating an all-night march, lay down to get a little sleep, but I was too excited and passed the time playing naughts and crosses with O'Rourke in the dark. Some time after ten P.M. we were ordered into formation and set off on the Stevensburg Road heading south. The march was exhilarating at first, as the night air was cool and refreshing, and the anticipation of battle made my heart pound for joy, but after two hours we had made only a few miles and the damp air began to make my shoulders ache. We rested for a short while around midnight, then continued on.

Marching at night was difficult. A dense fog made it dreamlike. My pack seemed to grow heavier with each step till I thought my back would break. It is a pain I will never get used to.

At first light, we came to an area of wasteland called The Wilderness. Word was that General Lee had withdrawn into the gnarly mess for cover, and Captain Sam had said, "Where

Lee goes we will follow." I cannot begin to describe this twisted wreckage of trees, thickets, and swamp.

We continued marching down the road till about sunup, when we heard gunfire off to our right. They moved us into position along a stone wall on the right side of the road. My company was first on the left side, meaning of course that we had our left flank exposed. Captain Trundee calls this position "in the air," which it isn't, but I know what he means. Being at the end makes you feel like your head is sticking up. It makes you feel insecure.

We sat in silence all morning, anticipating a Rebel attack, but other than random firing, which had become commonplace, we saw and heard nothing. The underbrush was so thick we could have been right under Confederate noses and not known it, unless they started cooking lunch.

Around two o'clock, a cannonade began off to our left, but at times it seemed to come from everywhere, even our rear. After a short while we could smell smoke and knew that shot and shell were setting the underbrush afire. This cannonade continued until almost six, when it stopped and was replaced by sharpshooter fire.

Night fell on my first day of battle. I still feel as if I am dreaming. I have not yet fired a shot. Between the march in darkness, the poor visibility of the Wilderness and the smoky air, the face of War remains hidden from my view.

I must close now, Cousin. I hope that May in Connecticut is as lovely as I remember it.

Love to you,
Cousin Matt

CHAPTER SEVENTEEN

Sheets of Ice

"But can't you imagine it, Mary? The whole Connecticut River Valley a giant lake, and the land around it covered with ice! Try to imagine it!"

Mary Talcott rolled her eyes upwards as she put on her shawl. I was trying to convince her that this evening's talk by the Reverend Edward Hitchcock was not going to be a long, tedious lecture. Certainly the Reverend Hitchcock was an old man, but he had made many famous discoveries and had many interesting theories. I was sure that he would be quite a lively speaker.

I was not disappointed. The Reverend Hitchcock was indeed very wrinkled and old, but his blue eyes sparkled with enthusiasm. His strong voice filled the room with thrilling images of sheets of ice, miles high, travelling over the land that I called home. As he spoke, I could picture the giant glacier scouring the peak of Talcott Mountain in Simsbury as it moved relentlessly southward. He described how it started to melt, leaving an enormous lake twenty miles across, where the city of Hartford now stands. As the Reverend Hitchcock explained it, the signs of Ice Ages are everywhere around us!

I thought about the rocky soil of our farm. Perhaps those rocks had come from far north of here, carried by the immense power of the ice sheets. And the beautiful rolling hills I had grown up with! Were they remnants of the Ice Ages? I was determined to ask the Reverend about my hills after the lecture.

But he was going on about something else: some strange footprints that he had discovered thirty years earlier in the sandstone of the Connecticut Valley in Massachusetts. These were in rocks much, much older than the Ice Ages that had just captured my imagination. The Reverend Hitchcock had identified seven different types of footprints, and he had at first concluded that they belonged to gigantic, extinct birds that had once lived in Connecticut. But just four years ago, scientists decided that the footprints were made by extinct lizards called dinosaurs! My mind could hardly absorb all this! How old was this land we lived on? I grew dizzy with wonder at the vast stretches of time he was describing.

Filled with excitement, I went up to Reverend Hitchcock after the lecture. "Bushy Hill in Simsbury and the Blue Hills in Bloomfield — are they from the Ice Ages too, do you know?"

"I'm not familiar with those hills, my dear," he answered quietly. "Describe them to me."

And I did. I told him how the hills near my home were almost all oval-shaped, how they had steep northern sides and more gently sloping southern sides. I knew this from all the climbs that Matty and Samuel and I had made as children. The Reverend Hitchcock listened carefully, nodding and smiling.

"You've just described perfectly what our Scottish cousins call 'drumlins,' my dear. And yes, we do believe that they are remnants left behind by the ancient ice sheets. What a clever girl you are to describe them so well!"

I blushed with pleasure. How wonderful to be listened to and taken seriously by a man so famous and wise as the Reverend Hitchcock. We talked a bit longer of the giant footprints that might also be found in Connecticut rock some day. And of his college, Amherst, in Massachusetts, where he had taught for over forty years. And finally, of a seminary for young women near Amherst, whose founder, Mary Lyon, had been his dear friend.

"It's called Mount Holyoke, Miss Allen. And it is attracting many young women like yourself who are fascinated by the natural world around them. Perhaps your father would consider sending you there some day."

"But, Mr. Hitchcock, I am learning so much right here."

"Of course you are, my dear. But how many others like yourself do you find here — so interested in natural history?"

He was right about that, of course. Even my friend Mary found my fascination with geology and Nature a little strange. What would it be like to have friends who shared my interests?

"We need more naturalists like you to carry on the work," he continued. "It's intensely interesting work, with all the excitement and marvelous developments of a romance. And yet the volume is only partly read. Many a new page, I fancy, has yet to be opened! And you could be one of the people who will do it!" He shook my hand and gave me a warm farewell.

The events of that evening and the exciting new ideas about time and Nature that filled my head afterwards kept me awake most of that night. Matty wasn't the only one having adventures!

CHAPTER EIGHTEEN

Spotsylvania Courthouse

Dearest Neely, *May 14, 1864*

It has been over a week since I last wrote, but it seems like a lifetime. Life is a constant struggle with hunger, thirst, and exhaustion, made worse by black flies and mosquitoes. It seems to me that the world is covered either in mud or blood most of the time. We are always hurrying to get somewhere and waiting interminably when we arrive. Worst of all, my tent-mate

Dickey is among the missing. But I will explain how that came about later in my letter.

When last I wrote we were back in the Wilderness. The battle there turned out to be a three-day struggle, which they say we lost, but I don't know how anyone could determine such a thing about a battle fought in dust and smoke and underbrush.

The Fourteenth fought bravely, although in three days we saw only sporadic fighting. Late on the second day, General Hobart ordered our division to attack but Colonel Carroll refused to follow what he thought was a foolish order to advance into the thick underbrush.

The Colonel was proven right. Within minutes, the Rebels were pushing back the attack all along the left side. Because we were still dug in behind our barricades, the Fourteenth was able to hold back the Rebels for about twenty minutes, allowing the rest of the division to retreat and re-form. Eventually, though, we were almost surrounded and were ordered to fall back.

During this battle I was so busy firing and loading that I cannot say what was going through my mind. I do remember bullets zipping past me, thick as flies, and seeing men dropping all around me, but to tell the truth, it seemed unreal. Time passed very slowly, but I just kept low and kept firing.

Toward the end of the attack, just before the fallback

order, our color bearer, young Henry Lyon of Company G, was killed. As he fell, he valiantly turned to Colonel Moore and handed him the company flag. The event did not immediately register with me, but moments later as I aimed my rifle, my vision blurred and I realized I was crying.

After we pulled back, we were relieved of duty and ordered to the rear for rest. As we settled down with fresh coffee, word came that the Rebels were attacking again, and we were ordered back to the front. By the time we were back in position most of the fighting had ended, but we spent the rest of the afternoon and evening waiting. I slept that night leaning against a tree, cuddled up with my rifle. It was a chilly night, made worse by the lack of a blanket. I did not sleep much but spent the night thinking about poor Henry Lyon and the others who were killed. I couldn't stop worrying about Pa and my brother Henry. I didn't even know if they were still alive.

I saw little action the next day. We did take some casualties from cannon and sharpshooter fire, but I did not see any Rebels. We held our position most of the afternoon. I understand that we were almost surrounded at one point by Rebels led by General Longstreet, but due to the dense forest we were fighting in, we were not aware of the danger.

Late in the day we engaged in a minor skirmish, but I was not with the front line troops at that time. One of my squad members, Willie Bates, was wounded when a piece of shrapnel hit him in the left arm, and I was assigned to take him to the hospital tents set up in the rear. I was disappointed in a way, but Willie needed me as much as the squad did. I am realizing that there is enough of this war to go around.

After the third day of battle, we were ordered to pull out of our positions. Most of the veterans thought we would be moving back north of the river, or even marching back to Washington as we had always done after a battle. But when we reached the crossroads, we were surprised to be turning south, away from Washington. We were heading toward Lee, not away!

"Toward Richmond and victory!" I cried, and a cheer went up among the troops.

"Our smooth-faced Molly is a man now," said Corporal O'Rourke, "a veteran, tested and true." He was teasing but he was also speaking his mind. I had been tested and had passed.

I wish I could report that we set up camp that night and rested, but sadly we did not. We marched that evening and most of the next day, sometimes backtracking, always hearing that we were about to go into battle. The night of the seventh we did dig in, and quickly built fortifications. This takes several hours as we have to dig trenches and individual holes called rifle pits. The rifle pits are always set several yards ahead of the trenches and are manned by sentries. The idea is to have a few sharpshooters out in front of your lines to watch for enemy advances and slow them down.

That night I was assigned to a rifle pit, as I had proven my marksmanship at the Wilderness. I was scared to death, since I was all alone in the pitch black. It is an overpowering feeling facing the danger that you know is out there, one that you cannot see or hear. Every noise brings on rushes of fear made worse by the long silence that follows. I found myself imagining that the entire Rebel army was advancing on my rifle pit. I was sure that single-handedly I was either going to win or lose the war that night.

On May 8th, we again marched southward, and the day was uneventful except for a minor skirmish late in the day. I say uneventful, but I have to tell you that a day spent marching in the hot and dusty Virginia countryside with a heavy pack and rifle, infested by all manner of bugs, is not anything ordinary, except it is becoming more so. Add to this the constant thirst and hunger and the endless rumor of battle. This type of warfare is nothing like I expected.

May 9th was more of the same. Late in the day we crossed the Po river and started to dig in, but soon we were ordered to fall back to the north side of the river. We crossed and recrossed the river a total of four times in eight hours, which meant that not only were we wet and cold, but we did not get any sleep that night.

The next morning we crossed the Po for the fifth time, and the order came for us to move up. As we advanced through the woods we were hit by a barrage of shot and shell so thick I was sure we would all be killed. Somehow, despite fear and sodden clothing, we kept moving forward. We had each been supplied with seventy rounds of ammunition, but as we reached the enemy lines, I realized I was out. I had fired all seventy rounds! I quickly sensed that I was not alone, and after a minute of confusion, all of us gladly obeyed the order to fall back. It was then that we discovered that Dickey and several others were no longer with us. I wanted to look for Dickey but was ordered to stay put. After we were resupplied, we dug in and had some hot food, for the first time in several days.

After several days of marching through dust, I began to pray that I never see dust again, and of course my prayers were answered. For the last four days it has rained almost nonstop. I have wallowed through so much mud that I have begun to pray for the dust again, even though I think my lungs could not stand much more of it.

We haven't done much marching lately, as we have been engaged in another battle. We are now positioned near the village of Spotsylvania Courthouse, having seen some terrible fighting the last two days. I cannot begin to describe it to you, as I am much too tired of war at this point, and my real desire is to forget it all. Perhaps sometime when I have had a hundred nights' sleep and a hundred baths and a hundred breakfasts, I will be more willing. It would make your hair stand on end to have been here with me in the last few days. My romantic visions of army life have deserted me. At times, I wonder if I am doing the right thing. Losing Dickey has really shaken me. In my weaker moments, I wonder if I have the courage to face another battle.

I will write soon, however difficult that might be, for it is my only link to the world I remember and to you. And you are the only person to whom I can express my doubts.

My love to you,
Matt

CHAPTER NINETEEN

A Surprise Meeting

I had some free time before my drawing class, and I thought I should go to the bank to deposit the most recent bankdraft that had come from Matty. Her last letter was very much on my mind as I walked. Here in Hartford, it was a beautiful spring day, yet at this moment Matty was trudging through mud and dodging bullets.

The sun shone on Pratt Street and a light breeze blew my hair and my skirts into disarray. As I came down the steps of the bank, someone called my name, jolting me back from thoughts of Matty's plight.

I turned to see Tom Godard hurrying down the street.

"Tom!" I hesitated, gathering my composure. "How

lovely to see you." I hoped he wouldn't ask what I had been doing at the bank.

"And how are you liking the Seminary, Neely?"

"I love it. I'm learning so much! And the days seem to fly by." If only I could keep him from asking about Matty! I changed the subject quickly. "And you? How are your studies at Trinity?"

"Oh, they're fine. I'm beginning to think of becoming a doctor like my father someday, but nothing can be certain until after this war has ended."

"Yes," I answered sadly, "I know. But perhaps it is nearing the end." Another topic I didn't want to discuss! I was afraid I might let something slip about how worried I was, so again I changed the subject. "What are you doing in this part of Hartford, Tom?"

"I'm meeting Stuart Deming here. You do remember him, don't you?" His warm brown eyes looked at me searchingly.

I blushed with embarrassment. If only he knew how many times I had relived those dances with Stuart at the Phelps' party! Was there nothing safe to talk about?

And then came the question I'd been dreading. "And how is Matty doing at the Seminary? Why isn't she with you?"

Perhaps it was all too much — the worry about Matty, the lying to my parents, the surprise of meeting Tom, the reminder about Stuart — I don't know. I do know that somehow the dam burst at that moment. And I couldn't lie anymore, even if it meant breaking my oath to Matty.

"Oh, Tom," I blurted out. "Matty's not at the Seminary."

"She's not! Where on earth is she?"

"She . . . she's fighting in the War, and oh Tom, I'm so worried about her!"

His face filled with horror and dismay. "The War! Do you mean she's gone to be a nurse?"

"No, she's a soldier."

"You can't be serious, Neely!"

"I am serious! She's pretending to be a man! And nobody knows but me!" It sounded so dreadful, hearing it out loud for the first time, that I started to cry. Of course, it was just as my eyes and face turned red and blotchy that I saw Stuart Deming striding down the street to greet us.

As he neared, Stuart took one look at Tom's pale, horrified face and my tears and took immediate action.

"We can't be seen out here in the street like this," Stuart said. "Here, let's go inside." Taking my arm, he hurried Tom and me into the Congregational Church. We sat in a back pew and talked in hushed tones.

"What's happened?" asked Stuart, eyes blazing even in the dimness of the church.

I couldn't reply at first. Tom brushed his curly chestnut hair off his forehead, and gulped. "It's Matty

Trescott," he answered his friend. "She's run off to fight in the War. Dressed as a man."

Stuart's face fell with the shock of Tom's words, then immediately brightened. "What a girl!" he exclaimed. "I'd heard that there were some girls doing that, but I never expected . . . "

"But, don't you think it's terrible?" I asked. "She could get killed or badly hurt! I'm so worried about her."

"I'm worried for her too," put in Tom. "But I don't think it's terrible. It's just a bit surprising to hear that the girl you . . . I mean, that a girl you know has done such a thing. Have you heard from her?"

I told them about Matty's letters and where she was stationed when I last heard from her.

"She's in the real fighting now, from what you say," observed Tom, looking very distraught.

"What a girl!" repeated Stuart. Despite my distress, I must confess that I felt a pang of jealousy at his admiration of Matty's deeds.

"Now, Stuart, don't start thinking of joining up again," Tom said. "Our school work is very important, and we're doing our part."

What had they done, I wondered. Could Tom have been involved with the Underground Railroad, too? I'd heard rumors that there were people in Simsbury who were part of the Railroad — could it be the Godards?

"Well, it's clear we can't do anything about Matty, just sitting here," replied Stuart hastily. "May I walk you back to your school, Miss Allen? People will start wondering where you've gone pretty soon."

"Oh yes, you're right. Of course. I'd appreciate your company on the walk back to school. Thank you."

I grasped Tom's hand for a moment.

"I'm really glad you told me," he said. "I wish you had told me earlier."

"Remember," I answered, "Matty made me swear to keep it a secret. I wasn't supposed to tell you at all! But I will let you know when I hear anything further from her. In the meantime, you've both got to swear to keep Matty's secret too."

CHAPTER TWENTY

The Gates of Hell

Dearest Cousin, *June 2, 1864*

Again it has been too long since I last wrote. I would like to report that things have improved here, but in fact life has taken on a quality of sameness that would be truly boring if it were not so terrible.

Dickey Slocum was found, wounded but alive. He was captured temporarily but the prisoner unit he was in was hit by cannon fire and the guards and many prisoners were killed.

Dickey was hit by shrapnel and blinded in one eye, but he managed to crawl away with two other soldiers. He was found by the side of the road, in bad shape, with a serious chest wound. He might lose his right arm, but he is alive. I cannot allow myself to be too upset. I must go on.

When I last wrote we were still mired in the muck and mud at Spotsylvania Courthouse. As tired and downhearted as I was when I finished that letter, I awoke the next morning to the sound of a bluebird singing. At first I thought I was dreaming, but I soon realized that it had stopped raining, and when I got up I learned that the battle had ended. The Rebels had abandoned their position during the night.

But that did not mean we could relax. We were packed and moving in less than half an hour and spent the next several days travelling southward, in slow pursuit of a slowly retreating army. As near as I can understand, it is like a giant chess game. Lee moves. Grant counters. And so on, back and forth. It is interesting to think about, but tiresome to be one of the pawns, as we foot soldiers are.

On the night of the seventeenth, we ended up marching until sunrise. The next day, we were involved in a small skirmish, after which we settled in for a few hours of rest. That night someone shot a turkey and we roasted it over an open fire. It was burned in some places and almost raw in others, but it seemed like the best I ever tasted. We stayed in camp all of the following day, and I caught up on most of my lost hours of sleep.

The next day we were off again, marching south. We halted for coffee near the village of Bowling Green and after a short rest marched through the town. We were greeted by a crowd, mostly women and blacks dressed in Rebel uniforms, if you could call their rags uniforms. The women did not like us and were rather rude. Some of the soldiers shouted taunts at them, but I tried to imagine what it must have been like for these women to endure an enemy army in their home town, and how it must have felt with their men away. I sympathized with them. I began to see the war differently.

We marched on for two more days and finally ran into a large contingent of Rebels near the North Anna River crossing. We were ordered to dig in, which we did in record time. I spent an hour talking with O'Rourke. In this terrible place with all the death and confusion, he was a rock, unmoved by it all. He is tough and strong like my Pa. I am afraid that I like him too much. I am afraid to think about what can happen to those we care about in this war.

The next morning we were up and moving at four A.M.,

advancing on the river. We were supposed to take the bridge and secure it for the rest of the army. It took a few hours to push back the skirmish lines, but eventually we were able to secure our side of the bridge. The problem was that the Rebels were shelling the bridge and set it on fire. We were finally able to put the fire out and drive them off. The Fourteenth moved across the river to keep the Rebels from retaking their position in the hills above the bridge.

From our vantage point, we could see our brigade marching up from the north and the Rebels being reinforced to the south. We realized it was a race, and we would either be reinforced by our brigade or captured by the advancing Rebels. For an hour and a half we struggled to hold on, and in the end we prevailed. About five in the afternoon, we were relieved. We fell back and dug in, just in time to be treated to a thunderstorm. I have never seen such soil as they have here in Virginia. Ten minutes after it stops raining, it is so dry you think the entire countryside will blow away. Ten minutes after it starts raining, it seems like the mud is knee-deep everywhere.

Anyway, thanks to the rain, it took us until the early morning to finish digging in. We stayed at North Anna for three days, without food or water most of the time. The afternoon of the second day something funny happened, though. As we were sitting behind our barricades, two pigs wandered into camp from out of nowhere. I was so startled that I did not believe they were real, but Wilson and Stoneman were not so slow-witted. Within ten minutes, our unexpected visitors were being fried up for supper. It was surely a gift from Heaven.

We finally got orders to move up. We were supposed to destroy an enemy observation post, which we did, but suffered heavy casualties. Somehow I was spared. I could not help but think that if someone's aim were just a little off, the outcome might have been very different for me.

By eleven P.M. we were ordered to withdraw, and we moved back to the north side of the river. The next morning, I heard that the Fourteenth was down to only eight officers and 165 men. So many have been lost, wounded, or killed – my company has only nine left! How many more of my brave friends will I lose?

The next few days were more of the same – marching, digging in, a few hours' rest, a quick meal, then off again. But the closer we got to Richmond, the nearer we felt to a final battle, a win or lose struggle that could decide the war. On the 28th, we crossed the Pamunkey River, just seventeen miles north of Richmond. We dug in and waited all day. The next morning we marched another two miles, and dug in again. We did the same on the 30th and the 31st, each time a little closer, each time a little surer this was it.

On the 31st, we crossed Totopotomoy Creek nine times before we settled in. We were under constant fire. The next morning I was assigned to the forward skirmish lines, ahead of the rifle pits, but saw no real action. Today, we pulled out early and moved for several hours to our left in pursuit of a Rebel force. We reached a small crossroads called Cold Harbor about midday and dug in behind a big hill. We were shelled all afternoon, a sign that the Rebels are digging in for a big fight.

It has been raining for the last three hours and I am afraid it will continue most of the evening. It is so hard to sleep in the rain and it is not any easier knowing we will probably be in a fierce battle tomorrow. Kirby says it will be like marching into the gates of Hell and spitting in the Devil's face. I have come too far to worry about unimportant things like the Devil. It is the Rebels I worry about.

Some of the men are so concerned about dying tomorrow that they have sewn name tags on the backs of their shirts. I don't think I could do that and still have the courage to march into battle. Maybe we won't even see a fight tomorrow.

Brandy Station and winter camp seem a million miles from here, even though they are less than seventy miles away. You and Simsbury are even farther, and Pa and Henry seem like fading memories.

But I will go on. If I am among the dead in the morning's fighting, so be it.

My eternal love to you, dear cousin.
Matt

CHAPTER TWENTY-ONE

Under the Apple Tree

It was a hot July day. I was tired from climbing the hills above Simsbury to collect wildflowers, so I took advantage of the shade under the apple tree and sat down to think. So much had happened in the six weeks since receiving Matty's last letter. I gazed off at the hills that had been so tortured and scraped by the Reverend Hitchcock's sheets of ice. Then I glanced down at the rock near where I was sitting. Matty had buried something under that rock, and her letter had said to dig it up if she did not return. To dig it up now would mean that I'd given up hope. Would she ever return?

I thought back to the agonizing days in June when I

read in the newspaper about the battle at Cold Harbor. They described it as one of the bloodiest battles of the entire war — and Matty was a part of it! Every day since then, I checked the Hartford *Courant* for the list of casualties in the Fourteenth Regiment and held my breath until I was sure no Matthew Trescott was listed. Day after day, I searched those lists. And still no word from Matty.

Somehow, I had finished out the term and headed back to my family and the farm, dreading the first encounter with Ma and Pa. When I arrived, Ma threw her arms around me and hugged me tightly. It took her several minutes to inquire about Matty. And then I had to tell her the truth. I watched as her face registered first shock, then anger, then worry — all in a few seconds.

"Oh, Ma," I sobbed. "I hated lying to you, but what could I do? Matty made me swear not to tell. And I kept hoping she'd change her mind and come back, but . . . "

"Of course she wouldn't change her mind! That's the headstrong Trescott part of her. But you, Neely — keeping this from your Pa and me for so long! I can't believe you could do this to us! You've never done anything like this before!"

"I'm so sorry, Ma. I . . . "

"Well, I can't imagine what your father is going to say! He certainly won't take this lightly! But more important, how can we find out what's become of Matty?"

"That's what I want to know more than anything! At

least she's not been listed in the paper as a casualty. That's good, isn't it?"

Ma shook her head sadly. "Charlie Buell wasn't listed in the paper either. But the Buells just got word last Tuesday that he'd been killed at Cold Harbor. Newspaper accounts aren't always right, I'm sorry to say."

"Oh, Ma," I began but was interrupted by my father's bursting into the room.

"Neely!" he exclaimed happily. And then he saw my tears and the expression on Ma's face. "What's happened?"

And so I began again to tell the story of Matty's going off to war and my keeping her terrible secret for so long. At first, Pa's face turned red with anger as he sat listening, but then, just as with Ma, his concern for Matty overrode his anger at my lying.

"We've got to find out what's happened to her!" he said.

"Oh, Pa," I cried, rushing to his arms. "I'm so sorry I didn't tell you!"

"You were caught between your loyalty to Matty and your own honor, Neely. That's a hard place to be. I don't say you were right, but I do understand how you could do this."

"I blame it all on Matty," Ma began, but Pa interrupted.

"Now Phoebe," he said. "Let's not blame anyone.

These are hard times and people make hard choices. And she is Rachel's daughter, after all."

"Yes, yes, you're right, of course. The main thing is to find her now."

The mention of her sister Rachel had brought Ma to a halt. Perhaps, at that moment, she remembered how close she had been to her sister, and she made the connection to Matty and me. In any case, she never again blamed Matty for the situation. I think she even felt a bit of pride that Matty was a fighter and a Day woman.

Ma and Pa were concerned, however, that the rest of the town not know of Matty's disappearance. We decided not to tell anyone else — not even Jonathan or Benjamin — where Matty had gone and made up a story about Matty having gone to visit some Trescott relatives in Rhode Island. At some point, we might have to trust Samuel with the secret if it meant that he could be useful in locating her. Meanwhile, Pa would try to find out some news about "Matthew Trescott" of the Fourteenth Regiment.

And I would spend my days staring at the rock under the apple tree.

CHAPTER TWENTY-TWO

The Telegram

Worry was a constant companion as the days of July went by. Still I found myself drawn into the activities of the farm. On a farm, summer is the most important season. Everything is alive and growing. Everywhere you look is the miracle of life. As a farmer's daughter, I grew up knowing the joy of summer. It was my favorite time of year — long warm days, balmy nights, the beautiful green finery of Allen Ridge. The farm blossoms and the activity is almost nonstop.

This summer was different. Not the farm. It was all abustle — a blur of people and crops and animals. What was different was me. I could not get over the feeling that

I was responsible for Matty. A sickening dread hovered over me.

But Ma always said, "Life goes on," and so I kept busy weeding the vegetable garden, feeding the calves, and helping around the house. But nothing eased my feeling of guilt or relieved my worry. Until I heard about her — *from* her, really — I would not be able to clear my head.

The days went by, and still we heard nothing. In Hartford, I had kept up on the news of the day, at the Battersons' or at school, or from the newspaper. But here, all I could do was wait for the afternoon train to bring the newspaper.

One hot day in late July my solitude was broken. I was sitting on the side porch shelling peas when I saw a tall figure coming up the lane. I recognized the confident gait of Stuart Deming. At first I thought I was imagining him, as I had so many times in my daydreams, but when he waved and called out, I knew I was not dreaming. For a second my heart raced, but quickly my elation faded. Even his beaming face could not overcome my worry. In fact, it was having the opposite effect, as I was sure I looked as terrible as I felt. I tried to hide my discomfort.

"Stuart, how nice of you to come by," I lied. Well, maybe half-lied. It *was* good to see him, and his charming manner was comforting after all. "Can I get you some lemonade? I just made some an hour ago. How have you been? What are you doing in Simsbury?" I realized I was babbling.

"I'm just fine, Neely. A little dusty perhaps from my walk but just fine. No lemonade, thank you, but I believe I would like to sit for a spell." He removed his wide-brimmed hat and fanned himself with it. After a minute he began to speak.

"I'm spending the summer with my parents in Farmington, helping my father out in his office. I was up in Granby last night and on my way home, I got off the train here in Simsbury to visit you and Tom. I'm sorry about just dropping in with no notice like this, but it really was a spur-of-the-moment decision."

"Don't be silly. You are welcome anytime. I mean that . . . " I wasn't sure what I meant, as I wanted Stuart to feel welcome, but I didn't want him to believe that he shouldn't make his intentions clear. After all, certain things between a man and a woman are supposed to be formal. At least certain important things. This thought was rather embarrassing, so I changed the subject.

"Have you been to see the Godards? I didn't think Tom was in Simsbury. I heard he was off somewhere . . . " This line of conversation wasn't any better. I didn't want to seem too interested in Tom's comings and goings. If only I knew how to act, how to say things. I decided that silence was my best ally in this conversation.

"I got in on the four o'clock train and stayed at the Godards' last night. I didn't see Tom though. He's in Hartford on business." At this he raised his eyebrows and looked around. Turning back, he gave me a secretive glance. "Would it be all right if we took a walk? Somewhere private so we can talk?"

I was eager to know what he was getting at. I reached for my sunbonnet. "Yes, we can hike up to the orchard. The view from there is magnificent."

When we reached the top of the hill, Stuart sat down on an old oak tree that had fallen in a winter storm. He beckoned with his hand and I sat beside him.

"I have so much to ask you," he said, his deep voice turning serious. "I assume you still haven't heard from Matty?"

"No, still no word. I can't imagine what's happened to her. I fear the worst. It's been so long."

"Don't talk like that. Let me tell you what I've learned. Some of it is terrible, but please listen carefully."

I stared at him, mesmerized by the hope of news. His strong voice and confident manner were reassuring.

"As you know, Matty's regiment, the Fourteenth Connecticut, was engaged in heavy fighting at Cold Harbor, just a few miles north of Richmond. The Rebels were dug in on a low ridge, and Grant ordered an all-out charge, which was a terrible mistake. Our soldiers were mowed down in a hailstorm of bullets, and there were several thousand casualties in less than twenty minutes. It was horrible, maybe the most horrible battle ever fought."

I sat there, numb, unable to grasp the horror of his words. I tried to imagine the sights and sounds, the mud and blood of the battle. In her last letter Matty had written about marching through the gates of Hell, and this sounded all too real now. All her letters came back to me, words on a page describing the brutality of the war. Tears welled up in my eyes and a knot in my stomach forced its way into my throat, a burning lump choking my breath. I gasped for air. Stuart wiped my cheek with his handkerchief. The gentleness of his touch was comforting.

"Stuart, is she . . . ?" I did not want to finish the thought.

"Wait, Neely, there's more. Tom has written to his father to get his help in finding more about Matty. So far he's heard that Matty's company was pinned down and unable to advance as far as the other units. At first this was a disadvantage, but after awhile they were able to dig in, so they were in a strong position to protect the retreat of the other soldiers. We've learned that their casualty rate was much lower than other Union troops. Doctor Godard was even able to talk to a Corporal Geisenheimer from Matty's unit, who remembers seeing her as late as around one o'clock in the afternoon. Geisenheimer said that she — I mean he, since he doesn't know the truth about Matty — survived the heavy fighting."

"But where is she then?"

"Well, that I can't answer. Yet. Tom's theory is that if she were killed or seriously wounded, we would know by now. So it seems possible that if she were only slightly wounded, you know, a flesh wound or just a broken finger or something like that . . . well, Tom thinks that maybe she was able to get herself to a hospital area and give a false name. I think it makes sense. It covers almost all the rational possibilities."

"Except one?"

"Well yes, but . . . "

"She may be captured, Stuart. I know that. You don't have to hide it from me."

"Well, if she's captured, at least she's still alive. This war can't last much longer. The important thing is that it seems unlikely she is dead."

"She's not dead, Stuart. I know she's not dead. If I know anything, it's that Matty is alive."

After that, Stuart was a regular visitor at the Allen farm, always finding excuses to stop by. Ma and Pa were quite taken with him, and Ma was especially pleased when he complimented her cooking. I think it did everyone good to have Stuart's lively influence around. Even Samuel, usually so cynical, seemed to like him.

It was during one of Stuart's visits that Tom Godard arrived with the news. We had just finished a fine supper and were settling onto the front porch when a buggy came speeding up the lane. Tom jumped out and raced up the walk, looking as if he were being chased by the devil himself. As Pa stood up to welcome him and offer his hand, Tom waved a telegram.

"I've got news, everyone! Father has found her at a

hospital in Washington! She's hurt, but she's alive. Matty's alive!"

Everyone reacted at once. Jonathan and Benjamin began to ask questions. Samuel and Pa tried to silence them, while asking Tom for more information. Ma was praising God for Matty's deliverance. Tom and Stuart were congratulating each other on the success of their efforts.

But I said nothing. Tom's words still echoed in my ears: "Matty's alive!"

CHAPTER TWENTY-THREE

Homecoming

It was a happy day on the Allen farm. August was almost over. The long hot summer days on Allen Ridge were yielding to the cool beauty of fall. Already the ridge was dotted with reds and yellows. In the orchard the songs of bluebirds were being replaced by the screeches of foraging crows and red-winged blackbirds. In the forest, the gray squirrels were gathering nuts and seeds.

Late summer brought a similar bustle for the human occupants of Allen Farm. But today there was a special kind of emotion and activity, for today Matty was coming home.

I was silent all that morning, oblivious to the excitement

around me. Little was said at breakfast of the anticipated reunion, and Ma did not even ask me to help with the kitchen work afterwards. While Pa was hitching up the team, and the boys were clearing the table, I went to my room.

I sat on my bed holding Matty's letters in my hands. I was almost afraid to see her after all this time. I knew that she had not been badly wounded, and that she was healing well, but I was worried. Would she still be Matty? Had the War changed her?

The ride to town was quiet, and I was glad that we did not meet any neighbors along the way. Pa did not try to make conversation or "cheer me up," as he so often did when I was a little girl, and I was relieved. Since my return from Hartford, he had treated me differently. More like a grown-up. I appreciated his silence that morning.

Arriving at the Simsbury station, we secured the rig and walked up the plank walkway to the front of the station. Pa went inside to check the arrival time, and I paced nervously back and forth, trying not to look down the tracks at the speck on the horizon where I knew the train would appear. For a brief instant I remembered all of our comings and goings: that April morning long ago when her family left for Kansas, the cold December (was it really just last winter?) when she had breezed back into our lives, and our last parting in February, when she had brashly disappeared into the crowd at the Hartford train station. Pacing and thinking were not what I needed. What I needed was for Matty's train to arrive. What I needed was to see the shining face of my cousin, my friend, my sister. What I needed was a hug, and a smile.

I was so lost in thought, at first I did not hear the train, or respond to the nudge that Pa gave me. The sound of the shrill train whistle nearly caused me to jump out of my skin. But it also melted my fears and nervousness. The next thing I knew I was running along the platform waving, and suddenly the train was motionless — and there was Matty, her arm in a sling, stepping down to the platform. For a second, we just stared at each other, not wanting the moment to end. The next moment we were like two kids, running and jumping, and shouting. We fairly collapsed on the platform, amidst hugs and tears. Matty was home, and safe, and with me again, where she belonged.

We were quiet on the ride home, content to be together. As the wagon pulled into the drive, the rest of the Allens rushed out of the house to greet us. Tom Godard hung back on the porch. Ma was the first to reach the wagon. She threw her arms around Matty and hugged her. Tears streamed down her cheeks.

"Were you really in battle, Matty?" asked Benjamin, jumping up and down. "Did you have a real rifle? Did you shoot anyone? Were you scared?"

"Yes, I was really in battle. And yes, I was scared. All soldiers are scared in battle. It's only natural to be afraid when your life is in danger."

"You are a real hero," put in Jonathan, helping her up the walk. "Simsbury's finest. We should have a parade for you."

"No," said Pa. "No parades for Matty. Her story must remain our secret. She'll have to be a hero in our family only."

"Your Pa is right, Jonathan," agreed Matty, her gaunt face serious. She sat down slowly on the porch swing. "Except that I don't think I am a hero. I was just a soldier, doing my job. I suppose all soldiers who do their jobs are heroes in a way, but one thing I learned in the hospital is that the real heroes are not the ones who take life but the ones who save it. Doctors and nurses."

"Father tells me you got interested in working in the hospital while you were there," said Tom, as he joined her on the swing. "He said you were good with the wounded. He thinks you would make a fine nurse."

Matty smiled at him but was oddly silent.

"This war has gone on too long," sighed Ma. "Too many have died, too many have suffered. We are lucky to have you back with us, child."

"Lee can't hold out much longer," stated Samuel boldly. "He's dug in at Petersburg, but Grant is slowly trenching his way around the southern flank, and soon Lee will have to fight it out or turn and run." He looked proud of himself.

"Why Samuel Allen," said Matty with a grin, shaking her close-cropped curls. "I can't believe that this war has finally attracted your attention. It is truly a great day if you have become patriotic."

"Well, someone has to carry on in your place." He smiled and made a face, but he was clearly impressed with his cousin.

"Tell us how you were wounded," asked Jonathan, eyeing her bandaged arm. "Did it hurt?"

"Now, Jonny, some things are better kept private," protested Tom. "Perhaps Matty would rather not talk about it."

"No, I don't mind. I was hit in the shoulder by a sharpshooter. We were pinned down by the Rebels for most of the day there at Cold Harbor. The morning's charge had been a disaster, bullets flying everywhere, everywhere men dying, falling, being ripped to pieces. The bullets whizzing by sounded like a hive of bees all around me. I don't know how I survived. Eventually I was able to move to my right and stumbled into an abandoned rifle pit. I spent the afternoon using my Sharp's rifle to keep a gun battery from firing its cannons. I must have killed twenty men or more. That sounds horrible I know — it horrifies me — but you have to believe me that when you are there doing it, it seems like the right thing to do."

Benjamin gazed up at Matty and clutched her hand as she spoke. Jonathan leaned forward intent on hearing every word.

"Anyway, the Rebels were planning to counterattack and were trying to move around to our left behind a low ridge. I kept hearing noises and was trying to lean out of my pit to get an idea what was going on, and the next thing I knew, my arm was numb and my shoulder was stinging terribly. I sat there for the longest time, wondering what to do. If I moved out of the pit, I knew I would be shot at again, and if I stayed where I was, I figured that I might bleed to death, or maybe be captured in the counterattack."

"That sounds horrible! What did you do?"

"Well, I wrapped my shoulder with my handkerchief and waited until dark. I even got off a few more shots, although I eventually ran low on ammunition. After I got out of the pit, I crawled in the darkness for a long time, till I was too tired to go on. I slept for a while and when I woke, I ran as fast as I could until I came to the supply wagons. I walked back to the hospital tents, purposely avoiding my own battalion hospital and doctors. I gave a false name and pretended to be too confused to answer any other questions. Since there were others more seriously wounded than I was, they assigned me a place to lie down in the corner. A nurse gave me some water, and I fell asleep again."

"But what about your shoulder?" Jonathan interrupted. "Didn't they have to treat it or operate or something?"

"I was lucky. My wound was a clean one. I had a nurse clean and bind it for me. I was up and around in a few days."

"And that's where Father found her, a few weeks later," Tom added, with great relief.

"I'm grateful Dr. Godard agreed to keep my secret," Matty continued. "During my weeks of recuperation, I worked with him, tending the other wounded soldiers. In fact, it was he who saved my friend Dickey's arm."

"Well, I'm glad you're home, Matty," Ma said, rising from her chair. "You can recuperate much better here in Simsbury."

"You're right, Aunt Phoebe. I'm lucky to be back home on Allen Ridge with my family." Matty smiled her familiar smile. "When do we eat?"

CHAPTER TWENTY-FOUR

"From Now On"

The September breeze felt warm blowing through my hair. I took the path up to Allen Ridge, enjoying the orange and yellow vista spread out before me. After an eventful few weeks, it felt good to be alone for a while.

Looking upward, I spotted a fuzzy grey-white blur between the branches of an old maple tree. What could that be, I wondered — a cocoon of some sort? My curiosity overcame me. Hiking my skirt above my knees and tying it up with my sash, I started to climb the tree. It had been a few years since I'd climbed a tree and I suppose it was not a very ladylike thing to do, but I had to know what was up in those branches. Sure enough, it was a cocoon, a kind I'd never seen. I sat looking at it for a long while, trying to memorize its features so I could sketch it when I got back to my room.

Suddenly, I heard voices coming up the path. Oh no, I thought. I don't want to be seen like this! What if it's Samuel or Pa?

Peering down through the leaves, I saw Tom and Matty.

" . . . not old enough for marriage," I heard Matty's voice say. "I'm only seventeen."

"You know that both of our mothers were married by seventeen," replied Tom. Then he added softly. "That's not it, is it?"

They were now standing directly beneath the maple tree. What should I do? I had already heard too much to scramble down from the tree and interrupt. I held my breath and clung tightly to the branches.

"But I have so many adventures still ahead of me, Tom!"

"I should think that you have had enough adventure for a while," he said. "Is it simply that you don't return my feelings?"

"Oh no, I do! Really I do, Tom! When I am ready to settle down, it will be with you, I promise. But not yet."

Oh no, I thought. How can she be so foolish?

Their voices faded as they continued up the path. I sat in the tree for a while longer, watching them walk away. Then I jumped down and hurried home to my sketchbook. But I was too excited to do anything more than a rough sketch of the cocoon.

Later that afternoon Matty and I climbed the hill to the apple tree where we had played so long ago. Though her bandage was gone, she still moved more slowly than the Matty I remembered, but her mood was as playful as ever. With her hair starting to grow back, she looked more like her old self too.

"Remember when we played pirates and made Samuel walk the plank?" she laughed. "Of course, you and I were bigger than he was then. I bet we couldn't do that now!"

"I guess he's forgiven you for stealing his clothes, hasn't he?"

She grinned. "A lot of people have forgiven me a lot of things lately. Your mother even told me she was proud of me."

"We all are," I said. "But Matty, it's time you told me what you buried here last winter."

"Tell you? Why not just dig it up? Here, let's use this stick to pry up the rock and . . . lend a hand, will you?"

Together, we pried up the rock and dug with our hands through the soft dirt beneath. Soon Matty unearthed a small wooden box and handed it to me. I opened the metal clasp that held it shut and took out a wad of tissue paper. Unwrapping the paper, I found a locket — with a miniature of Ma and Aunt Rachel inside.

"Aunt Mary gave it to me at the Phelps' Christmas

party," she explained. "I thought it was the most beautiful thing I'd ever seen. And it reminded me so of you and me. I wanted you to have it, if . . . "

"But now it's yours again, Matty. And you must keep it with you from now on."

"From now on," she repeated. "What do you suppose 'from now on' will be like?"

"I suppose this war will end soon, and we will all pick up the pieces of our lives," I answered. "Now that we know your Pa and brother are safe, we can all make our plans for the future. Of course, Samuel will be back at Yale, as arrogant as ever. I'm returning to Hartford for another year, and if I continue to do well, I may persuade Pa to send me to Mount Holyoke to become a real naturalist."

"And Stuart?"

I blushed. "He'll be back in Hartford, finishing his last year at Trinity. I've certainly enjoyed his attentions this summer. Perhaps something will come of us. But what about you and Tom?" I tried my best to look innocent.

"Tom asked me to marry him today."

"And — ?"

"I told him not yet."

"Not yet? But what if you lose him?"

"I won't lose him," she said with a defiant shake of her head. "He understands that there's more I want to do with my life."

"What could you want to do that's more important than Tom?"

"Well, I've been thinking a lot about the heroism of all those men like Dr. Godard during my days in the hospital. And I've also been thinking there's no reason a woman couldn't do that as well."

"You mean you're thinking of becoming a doctor?"

"Why not? They started a medical college in Philadelphia just for women more than ten years ago! And now they have them in Boston and New York, as well. My wages from the War should be enough to take care of the tuition."

I thought for a few moments about this. I thought about all the changes of the last year, not just Matty's but my own as well. "I think that's a wonderful idea, Matty. You would make a fine doctor. And I guess you've proved to all of us that you can do whatever you set your mind to."

"Yes," she said. "I've proved it to myself as well. And if I were to find that the women's colleges aren't good enough, I could always disguise myself and go to one of the men's schools . . . "

"Yes, you certainly could," I laughed.

Our laughter echoed through the hills. It was good to have Matty home again.

Matty's War Historical Notes

CHAPTER ONE

Allen family: Although there were families named Allen in Simsbury at this time, this family is completely fictional. The reader should assume that all characters are fictional unless otherwise mentioned in these notes.

Kansas Territory: Kansas became a state in 1861. The Kansas-Nebraska Act of 1854 opened up these two territories to the option of slavery, by a vote of the people. This concept, known as popular sovereignty, was very unpopular in the North and led to civil unrest in Kansas, as pro-slavery and anti-slavery settlers fought for control of Kansas in the late 1850s. Lawrence, Kansas was settled by anti-slavery people from New England and was a center of Northern support during the Civil War.

Union victories: After a number of embarrassing defeats, the Union armies were able to secure victories at Gettysburg, Pennsylvania, and Vicksburg, Mississippi, in early July 1863.

CHAPTER TWO

Hoop skirts: A hoop skirt was a floor-length full skirt, held into a bell shape with a series of connected circular supports. They were popular during the middle to late 1800s.

General Grant: Ulysses S. Grant had earned fame because of his impressive string of victories in the western campaigns of the war, while in the East, Lincoln had struggled to find a competent leader for the armies. In early 1864, Grant was called to Washington and appointed as commander of all the Union armies, east and west.

Wharton Godard: Dr. Godard was a real person who served as a surgeon in the Union army. His name is found on a monument to Simsbury's veterans in the Weatogue section of Simsbury. He died at some point in the war, and all the information about him in the novel is fictional.

Trains: In 1864, Connecticut's railroad network was extensive. The north-south line through Simsbury was the Canal Railroad, running from New Haven northward through the Quinnipiac and Farmington river valleys into Massachusetts. The major east-west line was the Providence & Hartford line, which ran through Plainville. A direct line to Hartford from Simsbury would not be opened until a few years after our story.

Thomas Godard: Although Wharton Godard was a real person, Thomas is a fictional character.

District school: There were nine district schools in Simsbury that went up to grade 8. There was no high school in Simsbury until 1902.

Seminary in Hartford: The Hartford Female Seminary was founded in 1824 by Catharine Beecher (see below). After Beecher left in the 1830s, it continued to operate, based on Beecher's principles. The 1863–64 catalog lists a total of 207 students from many different states. By 1876–77, the school was down to fifty students most of whom were local. It closed its doors in the early 1880s.

Catharine Beecher: Catharine Beecher (1800–1878) was one of the thirteen children of Lyman Beecher and Roxanna Foote Beecher. In 1824, she founded the Hartford Female Seminary. In 1832, she established the Western Female Institute in Cincinnati, Ohio, and later similar schools in Quincy, Illinois, Milwaukee, Wisconsin, and Burlington, Iowa. She was the author of works on religion, health, domestic science, and education for women.

Harriet Beecher Stowe: Harriet Beecher Stowe (1811–1896) was Catharine's sister. In 1824, she went to Hartford to study and later to teach at Catharine's school. She married Calvin Stowe in 1836. Her novel *Uncle Tom's Cabin* (1852) sold 300,000 copies in its first year. A later novel *Dred* (1856) also dealt with the topic of slavery.

CHAPTER THREE

Yale: Yale University, chartered 1701 as a college for men, had several homes until 1716 when it was established in New Haven. It primarily prepared men for law or the ministry and did not require a prior secondary school education in the 1860s. Yale undergraduate school became coeducational in the 1970s.

Damask: A richly patterned fabric, usually of cotton or linen.

Mine Run: A minor battle fought in northern Virginia on November 29, 1863. On the map of Matty's War at the front of the book, it would be just south of the Rapidan River, slightly west of Grant's position, marked 1.Camp.

Isaiah: *Three Centuries of Simsbury* by William M. Vibert describes Simsbury as "on one of the trunk lines of the underground railroad. . . . There are several accounts that point to the fact that Simsbury had an underground railroad station, but its owner has not been identified" (p.137). We have placed some hints in this novel that the Godards may be the unidentified owners. Vibert also records a farm hand named Mr. Cooper, a runaway slave who had arrived in Simsbury via the Underground Railroad. There is a recently (1995) published report, *African-Americans in Simsbury 1725–1925*, by Mary Nason, published by the Simsbury Historical Society, that documents a memorial monument to Matthew Cooper funded by Simsbury residents in 1915. According to Nason, there were twenty-eight African-Americans living in Simsbury in 1860, five of whom were children fifteen and younger.

Freed blacks: A name generally applied to former slaves who had obtained their freedom. Some were granted freedom by their masters, others purchased it or had it purchased for them.

Runaways: Slaves who had escaped from their masters and were seeking freedom in the North.

We don't have to worry about any of us Allens being in the War: It was possible to pay a fixed fee for a substitute to fight in one's place in the Union army. The substitutes were often recently arrived immigrants or African-Americans.

Abolition Society: Like the Underground Railroad, we are uncertain as to whether there was an abolition society in Simsbury. There was a well-known abolition society in Farmington, so we have stretched it to Simsbury and put Mr. and Mrs. Allen into it.

CHAPTER FOUR

Saint Nicholas: A fourth-century bishop noted for his gift of money to a poor man; St. Nicholas's day is December 6th. Made famous in 1822 by Clement Moore's poem "A Visit from St. Nicholas," Saint Nick or Santa Claus was part of Christmas celebrations in America by the middle of the 19th century.

Pettibone Tavern: The tavern is shown on the Simsbury map where it stood in 1869. The present Chart House restaurant occupies this site today.

Old Canal: The New Haven and Northampton Canal operated from 1828–1848. It was no longer used for transportation after the railroad was built.

Toy-Bickford: Toy-Bickford & Company, run by Joseph Toy, was originally a munitions factory, making safety fuses for explosives. Today it is called the Ensign-Bickford Company.

War profiteering: Because of increased demand during wartime, costs of goods rose sharply, so that manufacturers and store owners could often charge higher prices.

hearth: The floor of the fireplace, usually extending into a room and paved with brick, flagstone, or cement.

Ransom's: This was a large store in Hartford.

Cloak: A loose outer garment, like a cape.

CHAPTER FIVE

Phelps' House: Captain Elisha Phelps, a commissioner in the Revolutionary Army, was approached by residents of Simsbury, including the local Masonic chapter, who expressed their need for a meeting place. The result was that Captain Phelps built a typical four bedroom house — with a ballroom. Although it is unknown whether the Phelps family held an annual Christmas party, there is evidence that they did entertain. The house is still standing, located on Hopmeadow Street, south of the Simsbury Town Hall.

Quadrille: A quadrille is a square dance for four couples which consists of five parts. According to *Martine's Hand-Book of Etiquette* (New York: Dick & Fitzgerald Publishers, 1866), there were several rules that governed the dance and appropriate behavior, including prohibitions on conversing with a dancing partner and on competing for position in the dance. Martine cautions, "Young ladies should avoid attempting to take part in a . . . quadrille, unless they are familiar with the figures. Besides rendering themselves awkward and confused, they are apt to create ill feeling . . ." (p. 99).

CHAPTER SIX

Joseph Bartlett: *Three Centuries of Simsbury* by William Vibert, previously mentioned in the notes, says of Bartlett: "There were Democrats who took dissenting positions concerning the actions and policies of the Republican administration . . . For their stand in these matters, these men, led by Joseph L. Bartlett in Simsbury, were tagged with the epithet of 'copperhead.' . . . Mr. Bartlett maintained his residence in Terry's Plain to become a prominent force in state politics at the turn of the century" (p.138).

Historical Notes

Copperheads: These were northern Democrats who were opposed to the Civil War. They received the name from the fact that by opposing the war they were perceived as some as disloyal. Republican newspapers took to comparing the Peace Democrats, as they referred to themselves, to the poisonous copperhead snake, which often attacks without warning. The Peace Democrats took to cutting the figure of Liberty from copper pennies to wear as a sign of their politics — hence real copper heads were their symbol. (Note: this term was applied in colonial times to both the Indians and the Dutch.)

Jayhawking: Jayhawk, an imaginary bird, was a name given to the free-soil, or anti-slavery, people of Kansas, who fought against the "border-ruffians" (pro-slavery people) from Missouri. Both sides accused the other of violating the law by raiding towns and settlements of the other.

Stuart Deming: Although there were several Deming families in Farmington, Stuart is a fictional character.

Trinity College: Trinity College in Hartford opened in 1824 as Washington College. Its name was changed in 1845. It remained as a small liberal arts college for men until the 1970s when it became coeducational.

Underground Railroad: An informal network of white and African-American abolitionists responded to the Fugitive Slave Act of 1850 by expanding their efforts to help slaves escape to Canada and other safe destinations. The Underground Railroad was a series of routes and stopovers and included stations in Connecticut (including Farmington). It is estimated that by 1861 some 75,000 slaves had escaped with the help of this network.

CHAPTER SEVEN:

Not going as a girl: Approximately 400 women are believed to have fought in the Civil War disguised as men. Some enlisted to follow boyfriends or husbands while others did so for the adventure or for belief in the cause. Physical examinations were seldom made of recruits and women disguised themselves by binding their breasts and cutting their hair short. Often they were not discovered until hospitalized or killed, although some went on to receive pensions and were never discovered. "The Soldier Left a Portrait and Her Eyewitness Account," in *Smithsonian*, December 1993, has stories and photographs of some of these women.

Slouch cap: A soft cap, with a flexible brim that could be pulled down to disguise or alter one's appearance.

Joan of Arc: A young French peasant woman, Joan of Arc, led French forces to victory against England in the Hundred Year's War. In 1430, she was captured, tried for witchcraft, and burned at the stake. Following her death, she continued to be an inspiration to the French and lived on in legend. Said to be inspired by God, Joan of Arc became a heroic role model for nineteenth-century women. Loreta J. Velasquez, who served as a Confederate officer under the name of Harry T. Buford, referred to Joan of Arc as an inspiration in her memoirs *The Woman in Battle* (Richmond: Dustin, Gilman & Co, 1876): "From my early childhood, Joan of Arc was my favorite heroine; and many a time has my soul burned with an overwhelming desire to emulate her deeds of valor and to make for myself a name . . . like hers . . . among the women who had the courage to fight like men . . ." (p.37).

Great-grandma Day: This is a reference to Deborah Sampson.

King Philip: This is a reference to King Philip's War in 1675–76. The fighting began when relations became strained between Plymouth Colony and Metacomet, a leader of the Wampanoag tribe, who was known to the British colonists as King Philip. The war ravaged New England and eventually involved the Nipmucks, Narragansetts, and Pequots, as well as the Iroquois who sided with New York Colony. In Connecticut there was loss of both life and property. The Indians burned the fledgling settlement of Simsbury and the colonists destroyed several dozen Indian settlements. The war ended when Metacomet was shot and killed in a Rhode Island swamp by an Indian allied with the British. In the end, it is estimated that the English lost 600 men, 1,200 houses and 8,000 head of cattle. The Native American tribes lost 3,000 to the war as well as their power in southern New England.

Antietam Creek: A Civil War battle fought in September 1862, it is known as the battle of Antietam Creek in the North and the battle of Sharpsburg in the South. Robert E. Lee had invaded the North with the hope of winning a decisive victory and ending the war. He was met at Antietam Creek outside the town of Sharpsburg, Maryland, by the Union army commanded by George McClellan. Lee's army was defeated. It was the bloodiest one-day battle of the war and was the first major victory for the Union in several months. It led to Lincoln's issuing the Emancipation Proclamation.

CHAPTER EIGHT

Hartford *Courant:* The Hartford *Courant* is a daily newspaper, still published, which began in 1764.

Colt factory: The Colt factory in Hartford, a major manufacturer of weapons for the North, was severely damaged in a fire of mysterious origin on February 5, 1864. Surprisingly, only one man died in the fire. It was because of this fire that the Hartford fire department was established. The present Colt building, a newer structure, is now a Hartford landmark.

Bonus: Extra money paid to volunteers who enlisted in the army. The Federal government paid a bonus, states often paid bonuses, and even local communities could contribute to bonuses. The money offered was usually between $300 and $750.

CHAPTER NINE

Trains: See note on trains, Chapter Two.

Petticoats: Petticoats were underskirts, often full and trimmed with ruffles or lace.

Battersons: The *Circular and Catalog of the Hartford Female Seminary*, 1863–64, lists Clara Batterson of Hartford as one of the students at the school. Catalogs from the Seminary are available to view at the Harriet Beecher Stowe Center in Hartford.

Mr. Crosby: Mr. and Mrs. M.S. Crosby are listed in the 1863–64 catalog as Principals of the Seminary.

Tuition: In 1863–64, tuition was $37.50 per term, which included English and Latin. French and German were extra, and there were extra charges for music, drawing, and painting. There was a fifty-cent charge for the gym.

Room and board: A few students boarded with the family of the Principal at a cost of $162.50 per term. The catalog advised that board "may be obtained in a pleasant family, or with one or more teachers of the school at $3 per week."

Mr. Martin: Mr. J.A. Martin is listed in the 1863–64 catalog as the teacher of penmanship.

CHAPTER TEN

Matty's letter: The letters that follow have very few references to Matty's gender. This is in keeping with the letters of Sarah Rosetta Wakeman, whose letters have recently been found. In 1862, at age twenty, she enlisted as a private with the 153rd Regiment New York State Volunteers as Lyons Wakeman. See the *Smithsonian* article, mentioned in the notes for Chapter Seven, for photos of Wakeman and others.

Armory: A fortified building that serves as the headquarters for an army or militia group. It is also a storehouse of weapons and ammunition.

Washington City: This was the official name of the nation's capital in 1864. Rosetta Wakeman also got to be a tourist for a while in Washington.

Camp Wright: This was a camp located just south of Washington City. The name was found in a letter belonging to one of the authors of our book; his great-great-great-grandmother received the letter from her son in 1862.

Capitol building: The dome of the Capitol was not finished in 1864. Pictures of Lincoln's second inaugural show it partly completed.

Memorial to George Washington: This refers to the Washington Monument. Started in the 1840s, the funding was from private sources. By 1855, the project was abandoned for lack of funds, and the half-finished project stood for years. Congress took up the problem of funding in 1876 and the monument was finally finished in 1884.

Sharp's rifle: Modern, rapid-fire, breech-loading rifles manufactured in Connecticut, these were superior to any weapons the Confederates had. They were also shipped by anti-slavery forces to the settlers in Kansas, so that Matty's pride in a Sharp's is as a Yankee, a Connecticutter, and a former Kansan. (Connecticut was a leading manufacturer of rifles during the Civil War.)

Fourteenth Regiment: The Fourteenth was a real regiment, made up of volunteers from throughout the state of Connecticut. The Fourteenth was formed in August of 1862 and fought in the eastern theater, in the Second Corps under General Winfield Scott Hancock. Their first main battle was Antietam Creek, and they participated in all the major eastern battles until the end of the war.

The army was organized into various sized units. The largest was a corps, which consisted of about ten thousand men. A corps was made up of divisions, which were made of brigades, which were made of regiments. A regiment was divided up into eight to ten companies. The strength of each unit varied, and they tended to get smaller as the war went on. Thus the Fourteenth started with over a thousand men in 1862, added almost 700 new recruits in two-and-a-half years and mustered out only 234 men after the surrender at Appomattox. Attrition was due to death, injury, desertion, and expiration of term of enlistment.

Brandy Station: The main train station near Grant's headquarters. The 14th regiment received new recruits like Matty, on Washington's Birthday. See map at the front of the book.

The enemy: Lee's forces were camped directly south of the Rapidan River. See map.

CHAPTER ELEVEN

Drawing class: The 1863–64 catalog of the Seminary describes a Department of Drawing and Painting staffed by "distinguished artists who have received a European education."

Second division: The Seminary offered three courses of study: preparatory, regular, and supplementary. Preparatory could be begun at age eleven; supplementary gave particular attention to languages, music, or art. The regular course of study had five divisions. In division one, students studied arithmetic, geography, English grammar and composition, reading, spelling and writing, Latin, French or German, drawing, and music. We have placed Neely in the second division where she would be studying higher arithmetic, natural history, and American history as well as the subjects in the first division. In the third division, she would add algebra and further biological studies; in the fourth, she would have geometry, chemistry, geology, and astronomy as well as rhetoric and elocution. The fifth division included trigonometry, aesthetics, religious studies, mental and moral philosophy, and art history.

Natural history: At this time, natural history included the biological sciences (botany, zoology) as well as some geology. Physics was called natural philosophy.

Catharine Beecher: See note for Chapter Two. In an 1829 article, now in the archives of the Harriet Beecher Stowe Center, Catharine Beecher discussed her philosophy of education; this included a de-emphasis on memorization and an emphasis on discovering knowledge for oneself as well as learning how to reason.

Miss Goldthwaite: The 1863–64 catalog of the Seminary lists Miss Charlotte Goldthwaite as one of the teachers; she is also listed in the 1851–52 catalog. Miss Elizabeth Barry and Miss Ellen Palmer are also listed in 1863–64, but they do not appear in earlier catalogs that are held in the Stowe collection.

Benjamin Silliman: Benjamin Silliman (1779–1864) was a chemist, geologist, and physicist. In 1802, he was appointed the first professor of chemistry and natural history at Yale University, where he taught until 1853. Silliman's *Chemistry* was a widely used textbook in both colleges for men and seminaries for women. It was used at the Hartford Female Seminary, according to the 1852–53 catalog. In 1806, Silliman carried out the first study of Connecticut's geology. He also established the *American Journal of Science*, the oldest American science journal still in continuous publication. His son, also Benjamin Silliman (1816–1885), succeeded him as professor of chemistry at Yale in 1854. Silliman is listed as a visiting lecturer to the Hartford Female Seminary for the year 1864–65, but it is not clear whether it was the father or the son.

Edward Hitchcock: Edward Hitchcock (1793–1864) was a professor of chemistry and natural history at Amherst College in Amherst, Massachusetts, from 1825–54, and president of the college from 1845–54; he was professor of theology and geology until his death. In 1830, he did a geological survey of Massachusetts. He wrote *Elements of Geology* in 1840, then revised it in 1860 with his son Charles, also a geologist. Hitchcock was a frequent visiting lecturer at New England women's schools like the Hartford Female Seminary, and he is listed in the catalog as coming in 1864–65. Hitchcock will be discussed further in chapter 14.

Annie Allen: All of the students listed in this chapter were listed in the 1863–64 catalog as attending the Seminary that year, as well as Elizabeth Hunter of North Bloomfield, Ohio, Louise Cleveland of York, Wisconsin, and Julia Pratt of New York City. We were happy to see both an Allen and a Day among the students.

Mary Talcott: Mary Kingsbury Talcott (1847–1917) of New Britain is also listed as a student in 1863–64. Her notebooks and scrapbooks are in the collection of the Harriet Beecher Stowe Center. Her notebooks show that during 1862–64, she read books by Jane Austen, Charles Dickens, Victor Hugo (*Les Miserables*), and Walter Scott, as well as *Dred* by Harriet Beecher Stowe. Her scrapbook, from 1862, includes many newspaper clippings, chiefly poems about the war — including the one quoted in this chapter.

Report on attendance: The 1863–64 catalog states that a report of attendance, deportment, and scholarship would be sent to the parents or guardian at the close of each quarter (a quarter equalling approximately two-and-a-half months).

CHAPTER TWELVE

Latrine: A communal toilet, often used for camps and barracks. In the Civil War, these were often just pits.

General Grant: Grant arrived on Thursday, March 10, 1864, to take command of the armies.

Fredericksburg and Chancellorsville: Fredericksburg, Virginia, was the site of a Confederate victory on December 13, 1862. Chancellorsville, Virginia, was another Confederate victory, fought May 2–4, 1863.

General Pickett: George Pickett was a Confederate general whose division was virtually annihilated on the third day at Gettysburg (July 3, 1863) in a famous charge bearing his name. Pickett's Charge on Cemetery Ridge is considered a major turning point in the momentum of the Civil War.

General Hancock: Winfield Scott Hancock was the corps commander of the 14th Regiment. Hancock's troops were positioned in the center of Cemetery Ridge and took the brunt of Pickett's Charge.

Quoits: A ringtoss game, using flat rings of iron or rope that are tossed at upright stakes.

Annual beating at Bull Run: This refers to the first and second battles at Bull Run Creek (July 21, 1861, and August 29–30, 1862) outside Manassas Junction in northern Virginia. The Confederates won both battles. The history of the 14th makes reference to the "annual beating," ignoring the fact that there was no battle there in 1863, but perhaps the battle of Chancellorsville, near Bull Run, fought in the spring of 1863, might have been seen as part of the annual beating.

Shiloh: This was a two-day battle fought in southern Tennessee, April 6–7, 1862. It was Grant's first major victory. After being surprised and badly beaten on the first day, Grant reorganized and won a spectacular victory that virtually assured that Mississippi and Tennessee would fall into the hands of the Union forces.

Vicksburg: Grant's second great victory was at Vicksburg, Mississippi, where he laid siege to this important Mississippi River fortress/town in December of 1862 and forced its surrender on July 4, 1863. The victory at Vicksburg opened the Mississippi

River to Union shipping and effectively cut the Confederacy in half.

Chatanooga: Grant's third great victory, this key city in southeastern Tennessee was under siege from the Confederates until Grant took command in October 1863. By November 25th, he had turned things around and forced a battle with the Confederates who were defeated and forced to surrender. (It was from Chatanooga that Sherman was to take the main force and march southeast into Georgia, eventually taking the cities of Atlanta and Savannah in 1864.)

Company G: Matty's company, which consisted of about twenty men.

CHAPTER THIRTEEN

Normal School in New Britain: Founded in 1849 to train teachers, the New Britain Normal School graduated its first class in 1850. In 1933, the three-year Normal School became the Teachers College of Connecticut, authorized to grant a four-year baccalaureate degree. In 1959, it became Central Connecticut State College and in 1983, Central Connecticut State University.

CHAPTER FOURTEEN

Brigade review by Colonel Carroll: This was an inspection of the troops by the brigade commander, Captain Samuel Carroll, in charge of the Second Brigade of which the 14th Regiment was a part. Parade uniform was the dress uniform of the troops, their "Sunday best."

Stevensburg: This is a real town near the army encampment, marked 1. on the map of Matty's War at front of book.

If I do go into battle: This line is quoted from a letter dated April 13, 1863, written by Sarah Rosetta Wakeman, mentioned in notes for Chapter Ten. "I don't believe there are any Rebel bullets made for me yet" is from another of her letters. Like many soldiers in the Civil War, Wakeman eventually died not from bullets but from disease in 1864.

CHAPTER FIFTEEN

Collecting flowers: The character of Neely is modelled on two New England women who became biologists in the nineteenth century. One, Lydia Shattuck (1822–1889) became a leading botanist of her day; her lifelong interest in botany was sparked by an assignment on flowers similar to the one that Neely is doing. The other, a marine biologist after whom we named Neely, was Cornelia Clapp (1849–1934), who became one of the first women in America to earn a Ph.D.

Normal School in New Britain: See note for chapter thirteen.

CHAPTER SIXTEEN

Privy: An outdoor toilet, outhouse. These were often just pits; hence, Matty is digging a hole or ditch, to be used as a toilet.

Colonel Ellis's tent: Colonel Theodore Ellis was a real person. His tent was knocked over in a windstorm and the story is reported in the *History of the Fourteenth Regiment*, mentioned above.

Naughts and crosses: Tic-tac-toe. The naughts are the Os and the crosses are the Xs.

Captain Sam: This is a nickname for General Grant. Grant's grandfather was Hiram Ulysses Grant, and Grant himself had been named Ulysses Hiram Grant at birth. While at West Point, his name was incorrectly printed as U.S. Grant on the cadet list. Fellow students took to calling him "Uncle Sam" as a result of this error. Later he was called Captain Sam. Grant retained the "S" as his middle initial, using it to stand for Simpson, which was his mother's maiden name.

In the air: This refers to the fact that the regiment was the farthest to the left with no other forces protecting their left side or flank. The term was used in *The History of the Fourteenth Regiment*.

CHAPTER SEVENTEEN

Shawl: A square or rectangular piece of cloth worn to cover the head, neck, and shoulders.

Reverend Hitchcock: Refer back to notes for Chapter Eleven. Edward Hitchcock was a graduate of Yale Theological Seminary (1820). Before coming to Amherst College, he had been pastor of the Congregational church in Conway, Massachusetts, 1821–25. We have taken some liberties with historical fact here. Although Hitchcock was listed as a visiting lecturer for the year 1864–65 at the Hartford Female Seminary, he died in February 1864. For the purpose of our story, however, we have him visiting in April 1864!

Enormous lake: In 1822, Hitchcock recognized that the Connecticut River valley was once the site of an enormous lake, twenty miles across at its widest point just north of present-day Hartford. Many years later, it was discovered that the lake formed as the result of damming of the river by deposits from the Ice Ages. The lake was named Glacial Lake Hitchcock in his honor.

Ice Ages: From 1824–1840, evidence accumulated that there had been an Ice Age in Europe. In 1846, the Swiss naturalist Louis Agassiz came to Harvard University and began to find evidence of glaciers in New England. Agassiz proposed that the northern parts of both Europe and North America had once been covered by thick glaciers.

Footprints: The first dinosaur footprints in the Connecticut Valley were discovered in South Hadley, Massachusetts, in 1802. Subsequently many more prints were discovered in the Connecticut River Valley of both Connecticut and Massachusetts. The first scientific study of the tracks was carried out by Hitchcock, who identified seven different types of prints by 1836. He interpreted the prints as tracks of extinct birds. The idea of extinct species was controversial at this time as it seemed to contradict biblical teachings. In 1859, the prints were attributed to small dinosaurs. (The first dinosaur skeleton had been found in England in 1822 and determined to be an extinct reptile by Georges Cuvier, the leading expert on fossils of his day. The name dinosaur, meaning "terrible lizard," was coined in England in 1842.)

Amherst College: Amherst College in Amherst, Massachusetts, opened in 1821 as a liberal arts college for men. It became coeducational in the 1970s. Hitchcock was its president from 1845–54.

Mary Lyon: Mary Lyon (1797–1849) founded Mount Holyoke Seminary in South Hadley, Massachusetts, in 1837. Prior to that she had taught at several academies in New England and studied science with Edward Hitchcock at Amherst and Amos Eaton of the Rensselaer School of Technology. Hitchcock remained a close friend and supporter of Lyon throughout her life and continued his support of the Seminary after her death. The Seminary became Mount Holyoke College in 1887, which still exists — the oldest institution for the higher education of women in the United States. Because of its strong emphasis on science from its founding, Mount Holyoke has always attracted women interested in science and has graduated a large proportion of America's women scientists.

Romance: Reverend Hitchcock uses the word *romance* here to mean a book of romantic fiction or a novel. His words to Neely, from "having all the excitement" to "will yet be opened," are a direct quote from his book *Ichnology of Massachusetts*, published in 1858.

CHAPTER EIGHTEEN

General Hobart: Hobart was a real person, who commanded the Third Division. He is referred to as "General Hobart" in the *History of the Fourteenth Regiment*, but other references list him as General J.H. Hobart Ward.

Colonel Carroll: Previously mentioned in Chapter Fourteen, Colonel Carroll did refuse to attack and as a result was in position to save the retreating soldiers of the Third Division.

Henry Lyon and Colonel Moore: These are both real people. Colonel Moore was Samuel Moore. This event really happened and is recorded in the *History of the Fourteenth Regiment*.

General Longstreet: James Longstreet was a Confederate corps commander.

Crossed and recrossed the river: The history of the 14th is full of accounts of the troops' wasted efforts, such as digging in and preparing for an imminent battle, only to be told to abandon the position and march to a new location, and dig in again. The campaign from the Wilderness to Cold Harbor was one of move and countermove, as the generals played a giant game of chess with each other. As a part of this, the 14th did cross and recross the Po River several times in one day.

It would make your hair stand on end: This is also quoted from one of Rosetta Wakeman's letters.

CHAPTER NINETEEN

Becoming a doctor: During the colonial period, in order to be a doctor, a man had to be at least twenty-four years old and hold a bachelor's degree. By the War of 1812, there were seven medical colleges in the United States, all associated with universities. Twenty-six new schools were established between 1812 and 1840, and forty-seven more between 1840–77. These new colleges were often started by a few physicians in a rural village and demanded no prior study of science or mathematics. Often doctors received their degree within a year. By the Civil War era, most men who attended medical school had not previously attended college. Medical education was weak and there was widespread suspicion of doctors. At a convention held in New Haven in 1860, it was proposed that there be three years of study (after a suitable preliminary education) followed by four months of clinical study in a hospital, but the Civil War intervened in the move for reform of medical education. As late as 1910, Yale Medical School required only two years of college prior to entrance; previously only a high school degree was needed. Professionalization of medicine and standardization of entrance requirements began after 1913 with the publication of the Flexnor Report.

CHAPTER TWENTY

Bowling Green: This is a real town, just north of the North Anna crossing. This incident is recorded in *The History of the Fourteenth Regiment.*

Cold Harbor: An insignificant crossroads north of Richmond, it was named for the fact that the tavern there did not serve warm food, hence it was a "cold harbor." Grant was caught off-guard, allowing the Confederates to dig in, forcing him to attack a six-mile fortified position, which was disastrous. At Cold Harbor, the Union suffered 8,000 casualties in 8 minutes, the most bloody action of the war. All references to the battle here are real, including the fact that some men sewed their names into the backs of their uniforms, fearing that if they were killed in a frontal assault, they might be unrecognizable.

CHAPTER TWENTY-TWO

Corporal Geisenheimer: The Geisenheimer family of New Jersey was founded by one of two brothers who came to the United States during the Civil War. The two brothers, both German Jews, were recruited immediately to serve in the army — but one served in the Union army and the other in the Confederate army. Both men lived to establish families, one in the North and one in the South.

CHAPTER TWENTY-THREE

Lee at Petersburg: After the spring campaign, the war in the east settled down into a siege at Petersburg, which lasted eight months until Grant was able to force Lee to retreat up the Appomattox River and eventually surrender on April 8, 1865. See map at the front of the book.

CHAPTER TWENTY-FOUR

Medical college for women: In 1847, Elizabeth Blackwell was admitted to Geneva College of Medicine in Geneva, New York, by vote of the student body, who meant it as a practical joke. Nonetheless, she was allowed to attend classes and graduate. She opened an office in New York City in 1851, but she had trouble attracting patients. The Central Medical College of New York, which opened in Syracuse in 1849, admitted three women among its ninety-two students. Notorious for unorthodox teaching, it split into two branches, one at Rochester that closed in 1852 and one in Syracuse that closed in 1855. Lydia Folger Fowler was the only woman to graduate (in 1850) from this school and practiced medicine in New York City for a while before moving to London. Cleveland Medical College of Western Reserve College admitted Nancy Talbot Clarke of Massachusetts in 1850–51, then reversed its decision to admit females, but allowed Clarke to finish in 1852. She practiced in Boston. In 1853–54, Cleveland again allowed women to enter at the discretion of the dean; Emily Blackwell, Elizabeth's sister, graduated in 1854.

Historical Notes

The world's first medical school for women, Female Medical College of Pennsylvania, was chartered in 1850. Founded by a group of Philadelphia doctors, many of whom were Quakers, this school existed for 120 years (except for a brief period of inactivity during the Civil War). Nineteen medical schools for women were founded between 1850–1895. New England Female Medical College in Boston was chartered in 1856 and was the first to grant an M.D. degree to a black woman, Rebecca Lee, in 1864; this school merged with the medical department of Boston University in 1874. New York Medical College & Hospital for Women was established in 1863. By the 1870s, medical schools all over the country were accepting women into their regular programs.

Disguise myself and go to men's schools: This advice was actually given to Elizabeth Blackwell, the first woman M.D. in the United States, before she was finally admitted to Geneva Medical College. She had been turned down by every medical school to which she applied.

For Further Reading

ON WOMEN AS SOLDIERS

Sarah Emma E. Edmonds, *Nurse and Spy in the Union Army: Comprising the Adventures and Experience of a Woman in Hospitals, Camps and Battlegrounds*. Hartford: W.S. Williams & Co, 1865. (autobiography)

Richard Hall, *Patriots in Disguise: Women Warriors of the Civil War*. New York: Paragon House, 1993.

Eugene L. Meyer, "The Soldier Left a Portrait and Her Eyewitness Account," *Smithsonian*, December 1993, pp. 96–104.

Loreta Janeta Velasquez, (C.J. Worthington, ed.) *The Woman in Battle*. Hartford: T. Belknap, 1876. (autobiography)

Julie Wheelwright, *Amazons and Military Maids*. London: Pandora Press, 1989.

ON CONNECTICUT HISTORY

Michael Bell, *The Face of Connecticut: People, Geology and the Land*. Hartford: Connecticut Geological and Natural History Survey, 1985.

Mary Nason, *African-Americans in Simsbury 1725–1925*. Simsbury, Conn.: Simsbury Historical Society, 1995.

John Niven, *Connecticut for the Union*. New Haven: Yale University Press, 1965.

Charles D. Page, *History of the Fourteenth Regiment, Connecticut Volunteer Infantry*. Meriden: Horton Printing Co., 1906.

Gregg M. Turner and Melancthon W. Jacobus, *Connecticut's Railroads*. Hartford: Connecticut Historical Society, 1986.

William M. Vibert, *Three Centuries of Simsbury 1670–1970*. Simsbury, Conn.: Simsbury Tercentenary Committee, 1970.

ON WOMEN'S HISTORY AND EDUCATION

Joan D. Hedrick, *Harriet Beecher Stowe: A Life*. Oxford University Press, 1994.

Jane Roland Martin, *Reclaiming the Conversation: the Ideal of the Educated Woman*. New Haven: Yale University Press, 1985.

Carole B. Shmurak and Bonnie S. Handler, " 'Castle of Science': Mount Holyoke College and the Preparation of Women in Chemistry, 1837–1941." *History of Education Quarterly*, Fall 1992, pp. 315–342.

Benjamin Shearer & Barbara Shearer, *Notable Women in the Life Sciences: A Biographical Dictionary*. Westport, Conn.: Garland Publishing, 1997. (See also Benjamin Shearer and Barbara Shearer, *Notable Women in the Physical Sciences: A Biographical Dictionary*. Westport, Conn.: Garland Publishing, 1998.)

ON MEDICAL EDUCATION AND WOMEN IN MEDICINE

Martin Kaufman, *American Medical Education: The Formative Years 1765–1910*. Westport, Conn.: Greenwood Press, 1976.